THE NUDE ON THE Cigarette CASE

THE NUDE ON THE Cigarette CASE

REGIS MCCAFFERTY

iUniverse LLC
Bloomington

The Nude On The Cigarette Case

iUniverse books may be ordered through booksellers or by contacting:

iUniverse LLC
1663 Liberty Drive
Bloomington, IN 47403
www.iuniverse.com
1-800-Authors (1-800-288-4677)

ISBN: 978-1-4917-0010-5 (sc)
ISBN: 978-1-4917-0011-2 (ebk)

Library of Congress Control Number: 2013913175

Printed in the United States of America

iUniverse rev. date: 08/07/2013

For William E. Unger Jr. PhD
Friend and Fellow Pipe Smoker

I have some friends, some honest friends,
and honest friends are few;
My pipe of briar, my open fire, A book that's
not too new.

Robert Service

INTRODUCTION

So . . . Why an introduction for a work of fiction? In particular, an introduction to a mystery where the leading character is a struggling private investigator in New York City toward the end of the Great Depression. Late 1939 was still a difficult time for millions. Fear of eventual war had driven defense spending up by almost ten percent but even at that, 17.2% unemployment meant soup kitchens, flop houses, and shelters were still the norm in every major city. Europe was at war and the United States was still 24 months away from the attack on Pearl Harbor.

But something else was going on, quietly, behind the scenes, never making headlines in major newspapers or news programs on radio. Walter Lippman didn't write about it and Edward R. Murrow didn't mention it in his CBS news broadcasts. That *something* was nuclear fission and the beginnings of the atom bomb.

Exchanges of information between mathematicians and physicists in the United States, England, and Europe continued, but in diminished volume between the western scientific communities and those under German control and influence, most notably Denmark and Norway. Because the United States was officially neutral, visits, even by German scientists, were permitted but limited.

In December 1938, the German chemists Otto Hahn and Fritz Strassmann sent a manuscript to the German scientific journal,

Natural Sciences, reporting they had detected the element barium after bombarding uranium with neutrons. They communicated these results to Lise Meitner, who had in July of that year fled to the Netherlands and then on to Sweden. Meitner, and her nephew Otto Frisch correctly interpreted these results as being nuclear fission. Frisch confirmed this experimentally on January 13, 1939.

Notified of potential military applications, Abraham Esau, head of the physics section of the German Reich Research Council, organized a group of scientists who met on April 29, 1939 to discuss the potential of sustained nuclear chain reactions. Soon, a second group was formed to study the use and applications of uranium, the second group succeeding the first. That second group was formed September 1, 1939, the same day WWII began with the Nazi invasion of Poland, and the German military took control of nuclear research.

The United States government had no clue. It could be argued that while maintaining an appearance of neutrality, the State Department didn't want to become involved with any overt operation that smacked of spying, though there may have been other considerations. The primary function of the FBI was internal and the OSS (Office of Strategic Services) wasn't formed till June 13, 1942. But the truth of the matter was that nuclear fission was no secret. Information between physicists at The Institute for Advanced Studies at Princeton University and their counterparts in Europe showed US scientists were well aware of nuclear potential.

Scientists at the Institute and others were also aware of the possibility that a bomb of extremely powerful force could be created. Among those concerned scientists were Albert Einstein, Leo Szilard, Eugene Wigner, John von Neumann, and Edward Teller. Leo Szilard, with Edward Teller and Eugene Wigner, composed a letter to President Roosevelt, signed by Albert Einstein.

The letter, in part, conveyed the following warning: "In the course of the last four months it has been made probable . . . that it may become possible to set up a nuclear chain reaction in a large mass of uranium, by which vast amounts of power and large quantities of new radium-like elements would be generated . . . This new phenomenon would also lead to the construction of bombs . . . A single bomb of this type, carried by boat and exploded in a port, might very well destroy the whole port together with some of the surrounding territory . . . I understand that Germany has actually stopped the sale of uranium from the Czechoslovakian mines which she has taken over."

This story, *The Nude on the Cigarette Case*, is about the search for an American woman courier who has been kidnapped and is being held until the information she possesses can be wrung from her and passed to Nazi henchmen in the United States. The woman is a scientist who poses as an art dealer, a profession that permits relatively easy travel between countries in Europe. This novel is fiction, not based on known facts but in supposition that nuclear information was shared by scientists without regard to national borders, and those who facilitated the exchange of information sometimes walked a dangerous path.

As a work of fiction, references to real people, events or locals are intended only to provide a sense of authenticity and are used fictitiously. Other characters, incidents, and dialog, are drawn from the author's imagination.

Regis McCafferty
June, 2013

WWII TIMELINE—PRE U.S. ENTRY

FROM MARCH, 1938 TO APRIL, 1940

March 11-13 1938: Adolf Hitler, Führer of Germany, is cheered in the Reichstag after announcing the union with Austria. Immediately after the union, Nazis began a brutal crackdown on Austrian Jews, arresting them and publicly humiliating them.

September 29, 1938: Germany, Italy, Great Britain, and France sign the Munich agreement which forces the Czechoslovak Republic to cede the Sudetenland, including the key Czechoslovak military defense positions, to Nazi Germany.

March 14-15, 1939: Under German pressure, the Slovaks declare their independence and form a Slovak Republic. The Germans occupy the rump Czech lands in violation of the Munich agreement, forming a Protectorate of Bohemia and Moravia.

March 31, 1939: France and Great Britain guarantee the integrity of the borders of the Polish state.

April 7-15, 1939: Fascist Italy, ally of Germany, invades and annexes Albania.

August 23, 1939: Nazi Germany and the Soviet Union sign a nonaggression pact and a secret agreement dividing eastern Europe into spheres of influence.

September 1, 1939: Germany invades Poland, beginning WWII in Europe. France and England honor their agreement to defend Poland and declare war on Germany September 3, 1939.

September 17, 1939: The Soviet Union invades Poland from the east.

September 27-29, 1939: Warsaw Poland surrenders September 27. The Polish government flees into exile and Germany and the Soviet Union divide Poland.

November 30, 1939-March 12, 1940: The Soviet Union invades Finland, but have a difficult time of it. Finland eventually sues for an armistice that cedes the northern shores of Lake Lagoda and the small Finnish coastline on the Arctic Sea to the Soviet Union.

April 9, 1940-June 9, 1940: Germany invades Denmark and Norway. Denmark surrenders immediately. Norway surrenders June 9.

Citation: Chapter 12: Mollie Panter-Downes' letter was originally published in the *New Yorker Magazine* on September 9, 1939, republished in The New Yorker Book of War Pieces (1947). "London Goes to War, 1939," EyeWitness to History, www.eyewitnesstohistory.com

ONE

Nighttime. December, 1939. Snow falling to mix with the gray slush on streets and sidewalks. In the defused light of streetlamps and shops it was a gray night in a gray world. I had just come out of Jimmy's bar in lower Manhattan after downing a couple double bourbons, no chaser, and was crossing the opening to an alley when two muffled shots rang out. Quick. Double tap. I stepped back, paused a few seconds, then peered around the edge of a building into the alley but saw no movement. It was then I spotted what looked like a pile of blankets about one hundred feet in. Nothing else. I pulled my .38 snub nose from my shoulder holster and slipped it into my overcoat pocket, my hand around the butt and finger resting on the trigger guard.

Keeping close to the building, I eased into the alley and made my way slowly toward the pile, checking each doorway as I went. Nothing. The pile of blankets was a man. A man in a gray trench coat in keeping with the gray world. He was in a fetal position, slightly turned to one side, his hat about three feet away and his glasses a few inches from his face. He was bleeding. A lot. Blood was running from under his coat into the nearby sewer grate, mixing with the water and slush.

I bent over and turned him slightly so he was face up. He'd been shot center chest. Twice. Through spittle mixed with bright red blood he was mumbling. He grabbed at my coat, pulled me close, and at the same time with his other hand, tried to reach into his inside coat pocket. "I must find the nude on the cigarette case . . . Find the nude on the cigarette case." Nothing more. He went glassy eyed and stopped breathing.

I looked over my shoulder. Several people had gathered at the end of the alley and I hollered for someone to call a cop. With my body shielding the view from behind me I reached into the man's inside coat pocket and pulled out a cigarette case. There was a picture of a nude on it and quite a nude she was. I pocketed the case. Curiosity, I suppose, but whether about the man or the nude, I couldn't tell at the moment. If I were to guess, I'd say the nude, but I'd check the case later and make a papal decision.

I stood and waited on the cop who arrived in about three minutes. I knew him to see him, a beat cop named Howard. Whether that was his first name, last name, or both, I didn't know. He stopped when he got to the body, then nodded to me.

"Dead?"

"Dead. Two in the chest."

"You see it?"

"No. Heard the shots as I got to the alley but didn't see anything except this pile laying on the ground. When I got to him he was bubbling but didn't say anything. Died in less than a minute." A lie of course, but I had the nude in my pocket and didn't want to give her up.

"I'll call it in. Wait here."

I moved off to my left several steps. "I'm going to stand in that doorway by the fire escape."

"OK, Grant. Nowhere else though, huh?"

"Sure." I wondered if he thought Grant was my last name or first . . . or both. Names, like history, seem to repeat themselves.

Max Grant, private investigator, always somehow stepping into someone else's cow dung. That's me, alright. Thirty five years old, just shy of six feet, dark brown hair and brown eyes, heavy mustache, and 180 pounds if I've had a good meal that day. Ex cop, ex credit chase man, ex car owner, ex steel worker, ex married, ex ex. Ex cigarette smoker as well, or trying to. I kinda gave them up six months ago and switched to a pipe. Went from three packs a day to one pack or less a week. Depends on how much of a hurry I'm in. It's also made a difference in climbing three flights of stairs to my corner office.

The light from a lone street lamp shown into the doorway alcove at an angle and taking the cigarette case from my suit coat pocket, I took advantage of it. It was an old case and an old picture but a beautiful young woman nude from the waist up. Inside the case were four Camel cigarettes and a folded paper. I unfolded the paper and took a quick look. I could have taken three hours for all the good it would have done. The first line read:

> *One kilogram (about 2.2 pounds) of matter is equivalent to E = 1 kg x (3 x 108 meters/sec)2 = 1 x 3 x 108 x 3 x 108 joules = 9 x 1016 joules.*

There was more but in the same vein with few words of explanation. I folded the paper, put it back in the case, and returned it to my pocket for further examination in my office. My math was limited to the general high school kind and the only joules I knew was a drunken Frenchman named Jules.

The rain had turned completely to snow and large white flakes were gradually covering the body. I shivered, not sure if it was due to the weather or the circumstance. I blamed it on the weather. Less than five minutes later Howard was back with another officer and Sergeant Belden, another cop I knew. Belden was a good cop but could be a prick of the first order. We got along, sometimes even shared information, but I couldn't say he liked me personally. Well . . . that wasn't quite true. He didn't like private detectives in general, so that qualified me for his shit list. I stepped out of the alcove.

"You shoot this guy, Grant?"

"I already told—"

"I didn't ask you who or what. Did you shoot this guy?"

"No." No sense arguing. I'd just move higher on his list.

Belden turned slightly toward the corpse. "How is it you happened to be in this alley?"

"Heard the shots. Came in to take a look."

"You packin'?"

"Yeah, .38 snubnose."

Belden held out his hand. "Lemme see it."

I handed my revolver over butt first and watched the Sergeant open the cylinder, check that no rounds were fired and then put it to his nose. He closed the cylinder and handed it back.

"Not fired lately," said Belden.

"Nope."

"I could ask you to stay and make a statement to the Assistant D.A."

"You could, but then you'd miss out on a double bourbon on my tab at Jimmy's Bar just down the block."

Belden looked at me, debating. The booze won. "Gimme your card. If the D.A. wants to talk to you, he can call you."

I gave him my card, turned, and walked out of the alley.

TWO

I took the subway home. It's a long walk from Lower Manhattan to Flatbush Avenue in Brooklyn even in decent weather. Not that I haven't done it in the past if subway or bus fare cut into my bourbon or cigarette funds. I'd been doing reasonably well this year, but 1937 and the first few months of 1938 saw me standing in a soup line more than once. Then in mid '38, several insurance cases with a ten percent recovery fee and a couple juicy divorces had prompted me to open both checking and savings accounts. I also hired an assistant to manage the office and occasionally assist with an investigation. Her name is Pepper.

My office on Flatbush is also my apartment. It's a corner set of rooms on the third floor of a four story building that consists of an anteroom, office, bedsitting room off the office and a bathroom that can be entered from the anteroom or bedsitting room. I kept the bathroom door to the bedsitting room locked for obvious reasons. The bath contains a recently installed shower stall, sink, toilet, and small closet. The bedsitting room holds a double bed, side table, wingback chair and a couple lamps. It also had a small GE Monitor Top refrigerator in one corner. The freezer section, big enough for two ice cube trays, doesn't work, but I rarely use ice anyway. It did keep beer cold, however. In all, a sufficient and convenient room. It's also cheap, or at least cheaper than maintaining an office and separate apartment. And it's only a ten step walk to work.

A word about Pepper. She's a Negress, or Negro, or black—I'm never sure of the proper terminology—but her name is actually Paula Brown. She and another young girl of the same age, also named Paula, but white, were raised in a foster home. The foster mother, who was Negro, nicknamed them Salt and Pepper to remove confusion if she called for Paula. Pepper is tall, slender, very attractive, in her late twenties, and wears a light gardenia perfume which is the primary reason I hired her. I'm a pushover for gardenia. The fact that she had two years at City College, is extremely efficient, and knows more about running an office than I ever will, didn't enter into the decision. Or at least that's what I tell myself.

Unlocking the door, I entered the anteroom, Pepper's domain, hung my coat and hat on the coat tree, and went into my office to the small cabinet set into a bookcase on the wall across from my desk. I call it my stash cabinet but the only things stashed are glasses, booze and tobacco. I poured myself some Wild Turkey. Two ounces or so. The "or so" meant another ounce . . . or so.

I made it to my desk without spilling a drop, sat, sipped, took the cigarette case from my suit coat pocket and looked again at the nude. I was in love. From the way she was posed, the necklace, her hair style, and the background, I made an educated guess the picture was probably fifteen years old and she might have been twenty or so when it was taken. That would make her about thirty five now and she couldn't have changed that much, could she? No matter—I was in love.

Opening the case, I removed the four Camel cigarettes, unfolded the paper and pressed it flat on my desk. The cigarettes stimulated a desire to smoke so I filled one of my pipes with Edgeworth tobacco and lit it. A mild, nutty aroma filled the room, and the taste was a nice counterpoint to the bourbon.

I read through the paper from beginning to end and understood no more than I had when I took a quick glance in the alley. I turned it over and on the back was hand written ***Hvis vi antager*** followed by another short string of symbols and numbers. I hadn't the foggiest idea what *Hvis vi antager* meant. It was in a language I didn't recognize, not that I knew many, so I decided to show it to Pepper in the morning.

She had a better education than I, or at least lengthier, and I suspected she might have bumped up against higher math and physics. The only bumping up against I'd done was against women, and education didn't enter into the equation, so what I concentrated on was the cigarette case. The guy in the alley managed to gasp out, "Find the nude on the cigarette case." He had tried to say something more that sounded like "sar" or "shar," but never made it. So, slim as it was, I knew where to start. Or better put, I knew who to start with.

But it was late and I was tired. I finished the whiskey, turned off the lights to my office and headed for the bedroom, pausing only for a short pit stop in the bathroom and to brush my teeth. I hated waking to the taste of stale bourbon. I also hated a lonely bed. It had been a while.

Oh, the urge was easy enough to take care of. I had my pick of a dozen working girls within a city block but all too often it meant a trip to the local clinic afterward. In this neighborhood, "clap" didn't mean giving someone a hand for an outstanding performance. And as some sage once said, a night with a whore is all passion but no compassion. Sums it up, I think.

THREE

She'd lost track of time but felt sure it had been only hours since she'd disembarked from the ship and not days. She checked her wrist for her watch. It was missing, as were her small leather purse and the old Gladstone bag that she'd traveled with for years. It was leather, large, larger than most Gladstones, but she had a fondness for it. She'd bought it at a secondhand shop in the Strand, and though she'd haggled over the price, she still paid too much. Nonetheless, it was perfect for her travels.

The last she remembered on waking was getting into a taxi to share a ride to Brooklyn with a man. It was raining and there had only been one taxi available outside the port of entry. The man whistled the cab up and seeing there were no others at the stand, asked in a very gentlemanly fashion where she was going. When she said Brooklyn, he said he was as well and would be happy to drop her at her destination.

The driver, shaggy and unkempt, glanced in the rear view mirror several times as if expecting something or someone to say something but then concentrated on driving.

They had gone no more than a city block when her companion pointed toward the window on her side of the cab and asked, "Wonder what that commotion is over there?" She turned and looked but saw nothing. When she started to ask where, a cloth was forcefully clamped over her mouth and nose. She struggled but it must have contained chloroform or ether because she passed out in several seconds. She came to on a cot in a small windowless room.

She sat up, put her feet on the floor, and was thankful they hadn't taken her ankle high, English walking shoes. They were soft leather with thick tongue and warm. Warm. That's when she noticed the distinct damp chill of the room. She shivered and reached for the gray wool blanket that had covered her on the cot. She wrapped it around her shoulders, pulled it tight to her waist and surveyed the room. It was perhaps ten by twelve feet with high ceiling, no windows, and faded whitewashed walls that had begun to peel. There was a small table with two folding chairs in one corner and a bucket with a wooden lid on it in the opposite corner. A privy, no doubt. A second glance at the bucket showed the wood cover was a bit short with an inch of space on each side. She grimaced. Lotta good that'll do, she thought. If I'm here any length of time it promises to get stinky. No sign of food or water.

Her face around her mouth and nose was tender. Probably a very mild burn. Chloroform would do that, she thought. She stood. Still a bit dizzy, she remained motionless for a moment. She pulled the blanket tighter around her, lifted it off the floor and walked to the door. It was metal with a sliding slot for viewing and hidden hinges. No help there. She shrugged, reached out her hand and rapped on the door with her knuckles. Nothing. No sound but a very slight echo. She walked back to the cot and sat.

Two minutes later, the slide in the door opened with a snap. Someone peered in, then closed the slide and the door opened. Two men walked in, both stocky, and if she wasn't mistaken, European. One lounged against the wall next to the door and the other came forward to the cot.

The one in front of her spoke. "I am Mr. Smith and my companion is Mr. Smith."

She almost laughed but didn't. Schmidt would have been more like it, she thought. She didn't reply, just waited.

"You are Sarah Bennett, am I correct?"

She pulled the blanket closer. "You have my purse and therefore my passport. You know who I am."

"We also know what you are, Miss Bennett. You are a courier. You have information we want and intend to get, but first, where were you to meet Hans Moller?"

They obviously knew enough that denying she knew Moller was of little use. She opted for the truth. "We had no established meeting place. I had reservations at the Central Park Savoy-Plaza. He was to contact me there."

Mr. Smith Number One nodded as though he accepted that, then said, "And where is the information you brought with you, the information you are to combine with what Mr. Moller has in his possession?"

"Information? I don't know what you're talking about. I brought a small twelve by twelve painting by Picasso with me for Mr. Moller and was going to negotiate a price with him. You have my bag. You know it's in there. Why are you holding me here?"

Smith ignored her question. "Miss Bennett, you are going to tell us what we need to know, one way or another."

With that, he nodded his head and the second Mr. Smith took three steps and backhanded her on the right side of the face, knocking her off the cot to sprawl on the floor. Neither man made any attempt to help her. She picked herself up and sat on the cot, her hand to her face. Both men moved to the door but Number One paused. "We have several ways to gain the information we want. That slap was only the beginning. But perhaps some refreshment . . ."

They left, closing the door behind them with a bang and she heard it lock. Her face smarted and a tear trickled down her cheek from her right eye. She realized she had to urinate, looked at the bucket, shrugged her shoulders, went over to it, pulled her skirt up, underpants down, and squatted. Then she laughed. No tissue.

Sarah made a second inspection of the room she was held captive in, paying close attention to the walls and floor. Nothing but a small grate in the wall across from the cot with heat coming out of it, and not much heat at that. No cracks or seams that indicated a plastered over door or a trapdoor in the floor. Smith and Smith had chosen well. The only exit was the door they had used. The door itself was interesting to Sarah. It looked new and she wondered how the room had once been used. The viewing slot was indicative of some sort of jail or prison but she could think of no abandoned jails in New York City. Then again, nothing but intuition told her she was still in New York.

She sat down on the cot again and pulled the blanket around her. Her stomach growled. She smiled. Her stomach might be almost as good as having her missing watch. She'd had breakfast onboard the ship that morning at seven o'clock before disembarking.

Memory plays tricks, of course, but she felt she'd only been unconscious for a couple hours, three or four at most. She gave that some thought. Let's say three hours. Split the difference. That would be enough time to drive to a nearby location, an abandoned building perhaps, in the dock area, and with minimum caution get her inside to this room. It made sense so she'd go with it till something proved different.

She knew what they were after: four small, thin sheets of paper, folded and sewn in between the two layers of soft leather that made up the tongue of her boots. She'd stick with her Picasso painting for Moller story, but if her two interrogators got into the spirit of things, she didn't know how long she could hold out. She might be able to fabricate a story they'd believe for a while, some truth, some fiction. Then again, why? She didn't think anyone would be looking for her aside from Moller. No knight in shining armor would rescue her. And of course, there was every likelihood they'd do away with her after they got what they wanted.

What they wanted brought up another thought. She was in her early thirties, attractive, her body firm and shapely from walking and trekking in Europe as often as she was able. The possibility of rape entered into the equation. Equation—that was funny. That's what this adventure was all about: shared discourse and equations between scientists in Nazi occupied or neutral Europe and the United States. But rape was a distinct possibility, if not for business, then for pleasure. She wanted to dismiss the thought but knew she couldn't.

The slot in the door slid open and one of the Smiths peered in, then closed the slot. The door opened and Smith Number Two came in carrying a large metal cup and plate. He walked to the table, set them down, then turned and left without saying a word. Sarah wondered if he was mute.

She moved from the cot to the table and sat down. The cup contained black tea and the plate held two slices of thick cut bread, nothing else. She wondered if the tea was drugged but doubted it. It wouldn't be if they wanted information. She lifted the cup with both hands and sipped. At least it was hot. It was something else as well. The flavor and deep amber color told her it was Assam or Assam based tea, probably an English or Irish breakfast tea. That small fact was interesting. It didn't fit with Smith and Smith. But it might fit with . . . .

For the first time, she gave some serious thought to the man who had offered to share the cab and who'd attacked and drugged her. His appearance was that of a gentleman, a world traveler, perhaps a businessman. A high grade tea would fit the image. Of one thing she was certain: he was an agent. Whether freelance or Gestapo, it made little difference.

The bread was crusty, fresh, and she savored every bite. She had just finished when the door opened and in came Smith and Smith. Here we go, she thought.

Smith Number Two took up his place at the door as before and Smith Number One approached the table. "I see you have finished your lunch, Miss Bennett. That is good. Please stand and remove all your clothes."

That was a mistake, she thought. "Lunch." That gave her a time of day or told her that it was at least midday. She made no move to stand.

"Miss Bennett, we can make this easy or difficult. Either you can undress so we can search your clothes and your body or Mr. Smith," he nodded to the other Smith at the door, "can remove your clothes. Please take my word, he won't be gentle."

She remained seated. Call it gut feeling, intuition, whatever, but she somehow knew these two reported to the man who drugged and brought her here. She took a chance. In a strong, forceful voice, she said, "Mr. Smith . . . As you say, we can make this easy or difficult. I may or may not have the information you seek, but the only way you will ever find out, I repeat—ever find out—is if I speak with your boss, the man who brought me here. I will tell you this: I am a mathematician and physicist and have a photographic memory. You will find no papers on my person nor in my clothes and if you torture me, you'll get nothing and have to answer to your boss for your failure and my condition. A condition, I might add that would render me useless."

Whether it was the tone of her voice or what she said, it was obvious Smith was startled. He stood looking at her for a full minute before speaking. "We will talk later."

He turned, and motioned the other Smith out the door but she spoke again before he closed it. "I want some tissue and more hot tea."

He paused with his back to her and she saw what appeared to be a slight shrug before he followed Smith Number Two into the hallway and closed the door.

She smiled to herself. What she'd told them was a mixture of lies and truth but it may have bought her some time. At the moment, she didn't know how much time or for what, but at least time to think. She was a mathematician but not a physicist, and though blessed with a good memory, it wasn't photographic. And they wouldn't find all the information she carried on her person. One thing not in her boots was a verbal message from the Danish physicist, Niels Bohr. Among other things, he said he would flee Denmark with his family if the Nazis occupied his country, and she was sure they'd pay dearly for that bit of information. Not wanting to move back to the cot, she remained at the table, waiting.

Smith Number One was back in less than ten minutes and he carried a tray. On it were a roll of toilet tissue, a small stainless tea pot, some sugar cubes, and several tea bags. He set the tray on the table and turned to her. "I am inclined to believe you, Miss Bennett. It would be logical. I am afraid, however, that because of your comments, your stay with us will be extended. The man you say you will give information to is unavailable for a number of days, perhaps ten or more. I will attempt to contact him later today or tomorrow, but I warn you, if he says to proceed, we will." He turned and walked out of the room, closing the door forcefully behind him.

As he was speaking, she had come to another conclusion: Whether she gave them information or not, they would kill her. That was also logical. They certainly couldn't let her simply walk away to the authorities. She could not only identify the Smiths but also the man who'd brought her here. No way were they going to allow that. She suspected, no, she was convinced, the man from the taxi was an American but head of a network of German agents. And though Smith Number One spoke very good English, there was a certain Germanic flavor to his sentence structure at times. She would bet Smith Number Two spoke little or no English.

Her thoughts turned back to Hans Moller. When she didn't turn up at the Savoy-Plaza, he might come looking for her, *might* being the operative word. How would he know where to look? Unlike most Danes she knew, he was a selfish, self-centered bastard, but he claimed to have valuable information to sell and had hinted it would be profitable for her if she could find a buyer. She wasn't interested in the money but wanted to get a look at the information. Little chance of that now.

She placed a tea bag and two cubes of sugar in her cup and poured hot water from the tea pot. Ah shit, she thought. No spoon. She chuckled aloud. I'll have to ask for one. Then more soberly, she thought, I hope I'm in for a long wait.

FOUR

Shit, shower, and shave, as the military guys say. It's a good morning routine to abide by so I did. Feeling better than I had any right to, I walked through my office, through Pepper's cave to the front door and opened it. My morning cup of coffee and two Danish were sitting outside the door as usual. I had an agreement with the coffee shop on the corner for morning deliveries. They billed me once a month and I included a tip for the kid who delivered. I took everything to my desk and looked at the cigarette case again while enjoying breakfast. I relished the nude and her hint of a smile, a knowing smile. She looked comfortable, as if she knew something even the photographer didn't know. When Pepper came in, I'd visit Jake.

Jake Resnick landed on our shores in 1921 from Russia as Jacob Ben Reznikov and opened a small photographic studio on Livonia just east of 98th Street. We'd met some ten years prior when I was a beat cop and just before he changed his name from Reznikov to Resnick. He said he thought Resnick was more American and would improve his business. I don't know if it did, but he was still in business at the same location and had picked up a sideline of dealing in antiquities.

Now, at almost 60 years old, with gray, unkempt hair and mustache, hazel eyes, and a slight stoop, he had enough wrinkles in his face to put a prune to shame. But his hazel eyes always held a twinkle and he had a wry sense of humor and wit that was quick and spontaneous. And he was a pipe smoker who always had a pipe in his mouth, lit or unlit. It was Jake who helped me pick out a couple pipes from a local tobacconist's shop.

I was still sitting at my desk finishing up the last Danish when I hear the door to the anteroom open, close, and something that sounded like a purse drop on the desk.

"Hey boss, you up?"

"In what way, Pepper?"

"Can it, Max. Are you awake?"

"No more that I usually am before ten o'clock."

She appeared in the doorway wearing a tan A-line dress trimmed in black and a single strand pearl necklace that was just a bit less than a choker.

"Geez, Pepper, you look almost as delicious as this Danish."

"What chu mean, almost?"

"I mean if I said anything more, I'd be in trouble. Come in here for a minute and have a seat. I have a tale to tell you."

I gave her the whole story, from the alley, to the victim's last words, to the cigarette case, and to the paper that had been inside.

She looked first at the case. "Fine looking woman."

"Yeah . . . I'm in love. How about the paper? Make anything of it?"

After studying it for a moment, she set it back on the desk. "My physics courses were pretty basic but it's about fission and a release of energy by combining two or more radioactive materials. It doesn't read as if it were something that has been done but more like a hypothesis or proposal. This paper was in the cigarette case?"

"Yeah, guarded by the nude along with some Camel cigarettes."

"You smoke the cigarettes?"

"Not yet. I'm waiting till I'm hard up."

"Stick with your pipe. Smells nicer."

"Take a look at the flip side. There's more."

She looked, then frowned. "*Hvis vi antager.* No idea. Foreign language on both counts, the comment and the math."

"I'm going to visit Jake Resnick. If anyone calls or comes in, I'll be back in a couple hours."

"OK, boss. I'll hold down the fort."

The bus took me east on Linden Boulevard but at 98th I transferred to another that dropped me at the corner of Livonia with only a block to walk. Jake's shop was on the far western edge of Brownsville, a predominantly Jewish district in Brooklyn and if not the toughest section of the city, it's certainly in the top three. Home of Murder Incorporated and with notable, if unpleasant personalities like Bugsy Segal, Meyer Lansky, and Dutch Schultz, it has a fearsome reputation. Lansky and Segal are still around but Dutch had gone to the big syndicate in the sky in 1935 when he defied the mob and ordered a hit on Thomas Dewey. Dewey was the special prosecutor appointed to investigate criminal connections between the syndicate and corrupt police and politicians. It wasn't Dewey who got Schultz, it was the mob. They were afraid if Schultz killed Dewey, it would bring the wrath of the Feds down on the syndicate.

Two hit-men, Mendy Weiss and Charles Workman were assigned to hammer Schultz and on October 23 1935. They nailed him and several associates in the Palace Chop House in Jersey. Schultz lived till the next day. The others didn't. Of course, there are lesser known but no less notable denizens in the neighborhood, Willie "The Fly" Williams being one. Second story cat burglar. But he's not known as The Fly for his talent for climbing walls. He gets the nickname from his ability to leap from roof to roof when on the run from the cops. They're still trying to figure out how he managed to leap an eighteen foot gap between two buildings on Second Avenue. Everyone knows what he does and who he is, but he's never been caught in the act.

The bell over the door tinkled as I walked into Jake's shop. He was standing at the rear holding a large picture frame, perhaps two by three feet, under a bright light, turning it this way and that. He leaned it against his desk and walked toward me holding out his hand. We shook.

"Something wrong with the frame, Jake?"

No, no. I just bought. Got a good price and it's gold gilt on plaster. Reasonably heavy, too. It's old and I was just checking for crazing. Wealthy dame from over on Sutton Place wants to frame a picture of some impressionist artist's work and asked for something fancy and expensive. This should do it."

"Who's the artist?"

"Beats me. She just gave me the measurements and told me to let her know when I had a frame. What brings you here?"

"A puzzle."

"I don't do puzzles. Wanna play chess?"

"Not today, Jake." I slipped the cigarette case from my coat pocket, without the paper and cigarettes that I'd left in my desk, and handed it to him. "What can you tell me about this?"

"It's a cigarette case."

I just looked at him with raised eyebrows that said, I know that already, schmuck.

"Okay, okay—" He grinned, paused to light his pipe, and walked back under the bright overhead. He turned it over several times, then opened it, pulled a jeweler's loupe from his shirt pocket and closely examined the inside before closing it and handing it back.

"Nice looking woman."

"Yeah, I'm in love. Anything you can tell me, Jake, would be helpful."

"Well, it's not sterling. It's nickel silver or what some call German silver so it doesn't have a hallmark. It does have a mark, however. Actually, it has two but one is an overstrike and the one underneath can't be made out. The top one is a symbol for the last letter in the Greek alphabet. Here, I'll show you."

He walked to a bookcase a few feet away and shifted several books till he found the one he wanted. It was a large dictionary, and he turned to the last few pages.

"Here, you see this?" He pointed with his finger to a Ω. "That's the symbol. It's the last letter in the Greek alphabet. I'd guess it's a maker's mark."

"Mean anything to you?"

"No, nothing. Or at least I'm not familiar with it."

"How about the photo of the nude on the front of the case?"

"Nice looking woman."

"You said that before. Any idea of when it might have been taken or where?"

"At first glance, I might have said Bellocq, EJ Bellocq, but this photo is posed. Bellocq took pictures of prostitutes in natural settings, but so far as I know, only in New Orleans, and for some reason, I think this may be local. Also, I don't think this woman is a prostitute. Fun loving, perhaps, but not a prostitute. Just a feeling."

"When do you think it was taken?"

"Late 1920s, maybe. Also just a guess. Tell ya what: go to the corner, take Grafton one block north to Dumont and turn right. Three doors down on the right hand side of the street is a photographic studio owned by Rubin Stein. He's also a collector of old photographs. Tell him I sent you."

"Thanks, Jake. How about a game of chess some evening later this week or next? I'll bring the bourbon."

"You're on."

FIVE

From the outside, Stein's photographic studio appeared to bc the same size as Jake's. Inside, it was twice as wide, deeper, and partitioned with four open rooms having different settings, one being a bedroom. The others were a living room, library-den, and one with an outdoor backdrop. There was a chest-high counter that ran half-way across the front office from the left and a desk on the right. A small, bearded, partially bald older man was behind the desk.

"I'd like to see Mr. Stein, please. Jacob Rcsnick sent me."

"I am Stein. How is Jacob?"

"He's fine. Ornery as ever."

Stein rose. With his left hand, he reached for a cane propped against his desk while putting out his right to shake hands. "And you are?"

"Max Grant. Jake and I occasionally play chess."

Stein smiled. "And drink bourbon, I expect."

I smiled back. "You expect right."

"And how may I help you, Mr. Grant?"

"I'm looking for information about a cigarette case I was given recently." I pulled the case from my pocket and handed it to him.

He took it and sat back down, a look of apprehension on his face, or so I read it. He opened the case and peered at it closely; then closed the case and looked at the nude on the front.

"How did you come by this, Mr. Grant?"

"Like I said, it was given to me. Why?"

"By a middle-aged man, thick set, balding, gray trench coat?"

"As it happens, yes. Do you know him?"

"No. But he came to my shop yesterday morning to ask about this case. He was particularly interested in the nude on the front and where she could be found. I think he may have already known her name, or at least her last name, because he started to say it, then cut it off. His manner was secretive and protective of the case. He removed a folded piece of paper and some cigarettes from the case before handing it to me and then replaced them when I handed it back. As soon as I gave it back, he put it in his inside coat pocket. How is it you have the case?"

I decided to tell the truth. I figured if I didn't and he knew anything worthwhile, I wouldn't get it if I fabricated some yarn. I had a sneaking suspicion he'd see through it. Jake would. So I laid the whole incident on him including folded paper and the fact that I'd pocketed the case before the cops got to the body in the alley. I also added that I was a PI and that Jake could vouch that I was an ethical one . . . most of the time.

He sat in silence for a moment after I finished but finally stood up, took hold of his cane, and moved from behind the desk. "Come with me."

We walked the length of the studio, then paused while he unlocked the door to a room at the back of the shop. We entered, and inside were rows of metal shelves with file size boxes on them, all neatly labeled and from what I could see, in order by year. His cane, tipped with a metal ferrule, tapped on the wooden floor as he made his way down one of the rows. He pointed to a box about head high.

"Lift that down and bring it to the table in the corner."

I set the box on the table and stepped aside while he lifted the lid and thumbed through the files. He finally found the one he was looking for, pulled it out, handed it to me, and put the lid back on the box before saying, "Open it."

I did, and right up front was a much larger picture of the nude on the cigarette case, but in this one, I could see almost the entire room she was in. The case picture had been cropped. I turned from the picture to look at Stein, but before I could say a word, he spoke.

"Her name is Sarah Bennett. Or was Sarah Bennett at the time I took the photograph. It may be the same now or may not."

"When was that, Mr. Stein?"

"1929. August 14th. It's written on the back."

"I take it you've looked recently."

"After the guy in the trench coat left yesterday."

"You didn't show it to him?"

"No."

"Why not?"

"I didn't like his looks or his pushy attitude. Told him I didn't take pictures of nudes and to try some other shops. I don't, by the way."

"Don't what?"

"Take pictures of nudes. There are some studios that do, but I never have, at least until this one. This one was different."

"In what way?"

"I was asked by a friend, a close friend. I won't name him because he now has a successful business in the city, but what happened was this: my friend was an art exhibitor at the time and planning a show in Chicago. As part of the show, he wanted to display some photographs and hand out souvenirs, something to draw some attention to his exhibit. He brought two young women, one being pretty obviously a tart, and the other was Miss Bennett. I took a number of seminude photos of each in various poses. Miss Bennett was reluctant to speak but I did learn she had or was obtaining a degree from City College New York and needed money to obtain a higher degree. I think it was in mathematics but not sure. I'm not even sure if the college she wanted to attend was in this country. I had the impression it was not. I also had the impression she was posing for the money, and that she had never posed nude before. I do know my friend paid her very well and I never saw her again." He glanced at the photo again. "She was quite beautiful . . . ."

"How old was she when these photos were taken?"

"I don't know. Maybe twenty-two or three. Let me ask you a question, Mr. Grant. What is your interest in this?"

"I don't know. It began with a dying man in an alley and a request to find the nude on the case. I don't have a client and suspect I should just let it go at that. Find some way to get the cigarette case to the cops without being nailed for obstructing justice, but I have a hunch there's a lot more to this and I'm just wacky enough to want to know what it is."

Stein was quiet for a moment. "Perhaps a game of chess and some bourbon with Jake would be safer. That man who came here and who you later found in an alley was not a good man, I think. He had the stink of evil about him. Also, though he spoke well enough, there was a hint of something foreign about him. Take the file with you if you like. Return it when you can. I can see you're going to continue to dig into this mystery. I wish you well but I don't think I will wish you good luck."

I walked to 98th Street to catch a bus back to my office, the file tucked under my arm. The vision most folks have of investigations, whether by police or private investigator, is one of adventure, mystery, and often gunfire. Quite the opposite is true, of course. It's mostly plodding from place to place, gathering information piece by piece and fitting the pieces together as one would a jigsaw puzzle, hoping to eventually create a coherent picture, albeit often one with a few pieces missing. With a PI, the term gumshoe is appropriate. With all the walking involved, one is bound to wind up with Clove, Blackjack, or Doublemint stuck to the bottom of one's shoe. In this case, however, there wasn't any gum stuck to my shoe, just a nude stuck in my head.

SIX

Pepper was standing in front of our one and only filing cabinet when I walked in the door. She half turned, saw it was me, and finished putting some papers in a folder.

"The DA phoned. Actually, it was an Assistant DA by the name of John Smith. Honest to God, that's his name. Said you were to phone him the minute you came in."

"Did he say what he wanted?"

"No, but he sounded pissed."

"He always sounds pissed. Got his number?"

"On your desk."

At my desk, I took the cigarette case from my pocket, opened the top drawer and placed the folded paper and Camels back inside before putting the case in the drawer. Then I phoned the Assistant DA.

"Smith."

"Max Grant. You phoned?"

"Yeah, Grant. I want you in here for a statement on the corpse you found yesterday and I want you in here now!"

"First of all, he wasn't a corpse till a minute after I got to him and secondly, I haven't had lunch yet. I'll see you in ninety minutes or so."

"Listen up, asshole . . . ."

I hung up. I knew Smith from back when I was a cop. He started out in the department about the same time I did but was ambitious. Went to law school at night till he got his degree and soon moved to the DA's office. He was a shithead then and hadn't changed. He could send a couple uniforms for me but I knew he wouldn't. By the time he got a black and white clear to make the pickup, I'd be on my way.

"Had lunch yet, Pepper?"

"With what, my good looks?"

"Now, that's a thought . . ."

"On my salary, I can only afford brown bags and I ran out of them."

"Hell, you make more than I do."

"I doubt that. You buying?"

"Yeah. Call the deli and order what you want. I'll have a ham and swiss on rye and a Coke."

We ate lunch at my desk while I filled her in on my morning visits to both photo studios and in particular, comments made by Ruben Stein. I also showed Pepper the file. There were several pictures, all semi-nude with one essentially a side view of the photo on the cigarette case. In it, Sarah Bennett was turned to the right and looking coyly over her left shoulder.

"Fine looking body, that, "said Pepper, "at least from the waist up."

"Yeah . . . I'll bet it's better from the waist down."

She poked my arm, laughing. "Lecherous bastard!"

"Speaking of lecherous bastards, how's Bo?"

Alexander Bowe is Pepper's live-in boyfriend and at a strapping six-three and 220 pounds, he's big enough to fill the doorway when he occasionally comes to pick up Pepper. I shook hands at arm's length the first time I met him, but he's a gentle lad who adores Pepper and treats her like a queen.

"He's fine. Working four days a week loading trucks at the dock warehouses. He'd like to get on as a longshoreman and in the union but you know how it is. There's a few negro longshoremen but not many. It's who you know and particularly who you know in the union."

"It'll change, Pepper. Probably not fast enough, but it will. Anyone who hires Bo will be lucky to get him. He'll give an honest day for honest pay."

"He gives a pretty honest night, too, boss," she said, chuckling.

"I can imagine."

"No you can't!" She got up and went to the outer office still laughing.

I pitched the sandwich wrappers, tossed off the rest of my Coke, shed my .38 and shoulder holster and put them in the small floor safe we kept in a corner of my office. The safe also held Pepper's .32 caliber Browning auto, a Colt .45 automatic and ammunition but I rarely carried the Colt. Too heavy, but a real boomer if one was needed. Pepper had a license to carry a handgun and knew how to use one but had never had reason to.

On my way out, I told Pepper my gun was in the safe and that I'd probably be a couple hours.

"If I'm not back by five, call our lawyer."

"We got a lawyer?" She was laughing again.

"No. On second thought, call Bo and tell him to break me out."

Assistant DA Smith's office was on the second floor of the Justice building, a cubbyhole two doors down from the DA's corner office that had four windows instead of one. Windows establish a pecking order. The cop that was my escort, an old Irishman named Murphy just a short time from retirement, tapped on Smith's door and we entered. I knew Murphy from years ago. Hell, everyone knew Murphy. He'd been a beat cop his entire career and trained more rookies than anyone on the entire force. If he had a first name, no one knew it. He was simply known as Murphy or Murph. When he had a year left before retirement, they pulled him in and gave him a desk job. They thought they were doing him a favor but he hated it.

Murphy stopped just inside the door. "Mr. Grant to see you, sir."

Smith motioned me to a seat in front of his desk and went back to scribbling something on a sheet of paper. Probably his wish list for when he became the DA. He'd never make it but he thought big. Murphy patted me on the shoulder, winked, and went out. I sat. When Smith finished his list, he looked up at me.

"So, Grant, why'd you shoot that poor sod in the alley?"

I didn't say a word but got up, turned, and walked toward the door.

"Alright, alright, you didn't shoot him. Come back and sit down."

I sat. Again.

He opened a file, pulled out a single sheet of paper and handed it to me. "That's Sgt. Belden's report. Read it over and tell me if you have anything to add to it."

It was short and covered the facts, including that my .38 hadn't been fired. It didn't include my offer to Belden for a double bourbon on my tab at Johnny's bar.

"Nothing, except the victim was still alive when I got to him."

"Say anything?"

I lied. "Mumbled something through the bubbles but I couldn't make it out. He didn't last thirty seconds after I got to him."

"See anyone else in the alley?"

"No, and I looked. Had no desire to get a couple pumped into me as well." I handed the report back to Smith and he pulled another sheet from the file.

"His name is Hans Moller, Danish, here on a temporary business visa. No idea what sort of business but he had a used round trip bus ticket to Princeton New Jersey in his wallet."

"Anything else?"

"Why the interest?"

"Curious. I found the guy."

"The usual stuff in his wallet for a foreign visitor. About fifty bucks in bills and some Danish money. Comb, handkerchief, change, one of those Swiss army knives, and a half pack of Chesterfield cigarettes. Also a small, pocket-size notebook, probably bought here. Couple entries on the first page but that's it."

He took a three by five inch leather covered notebook from the file and handed it to me. On the first page were the entries, JN—AE 10. And under that, a name that leaped off the page at me: Sarah Bennett! Something must have shown on my face because Smith asked, "Mean something to you?"

"No, not really. JN—AE 10 looks almost like a bet note at Aqueduct and I don't know a Sarah Bennett." Lying was becoming second nature . . . or maybe it always was. "Maybe an owner or trainer's name. She isn't a jockey."

"You play the ponies?"

"Occasionally, but most of my spare change goes for hookers and booze."

"Figures."

"Anything else?"

"At the moment, no. But I have a gut feeling you either know something I don't or you're more interested than you should be."

I got up to leave. "That gut feeling is probably the ruben you had for lunch."

The expression on his face told me I'd hit the mark but he didn't say anything. I went out the door, turned left and was headed for the stairs when I spotted Murphy sitting on a bench next to a water fountain. I stopped for a drink.

"How long yet, Murph?"

"Two months, two days."

"Counting them down, huh?"

"Not really. Just something I'm aware of. Been a cop 37 years and have no idea what I'll do. Walk the neighborhood, sit in the park, sack groceries. There's just me and the dog, and he's damn near as old as I am. Wife's been gone three years now."

Then, as on rare occasions, I had a blinding inspiration. "Tell ya what, Murph, after they pat you on the back and give you that silver watch, come around to see me. I can use an experienced man on some cases. Not full time mind you, but probably often enough to keep you from being bored."

His face lit up like someone had given him a free double-double at the local bar. “You mean that, Max?”

“I said it, so I mean it. And it’s not busy work. It can sometimes be ugly hours in ugly locations. Just let me know when you’re clear of this place.”

He stood, shook my hand, and grinned. “Probably the day after the silver watch.”

I left the building, hoofed it to the corner and caught a bus back to my office. I had some thinking to do. Princeton, huh? What the hell was in Princeton?

SEVEN

Pepper was filing when I came in. Not in the cabinet—her nails. I hung my jacket on the rack and headed for the stash cabinet. Not for booze but for a cigarette. I felt the need. I took a Lucky out of the pack, put a match to it, and inhaled so deeply my toenails curled. I turned to Pepper.

"I can see you've had a busy day."

"Oh yeah. Bo came by, we made love on your desk and then he drank the rest of your bourbon. You?"

"Delightful meeting with Assistant DA Smith. So delightful, I thought he was going to arrest me. I really dislike that bastard. Arrogant asshole!"

She chuckled. "Geez, Max, why don't you just say it in plain English?"

"He gets to me."

"Oh, I could never tell. Learn anything?"

"Maybe. What's in Princeton New Jersey?" I took another drag on the cigarette. My eyes watered.

"You mean other than the battlefield?"

"What battlefield?"

"The Princeton battlefield. George Washington defeated the British 17th Regiment during the revolutionary war and I lost my virginity in a stand of maple trees there, not during the revolutionary war."

I just looked at her for a full twenty seconds. "You know, every day around you is an adventure. I'll bet Bo can't keep up with you after two minutes of conversation."

"He don't have to . . . if you know what I mean."

"Jesus! OK, other than the battlefield." I crushed my cigarette out in the ashtray.

"The one thing they're really famous for: Princeton University. And the one thing the university is famous for is their department of mathematics and physics. Albert Einstein is a member of the faculty there in addition to several other renowned physicists."

Twenty second pauses with a stare were becoming a habit. "How do you know all this stuff?"

"Don't you ever read the paper, Max?"

"Not since the crash in '29. Well, that's not quite true. If I place a bet on a nag, I may pick up a paper to check the race results. Might read the comics then as well."

"Ya know, boss, it might be a smart move if you'd pick up a newspaper at least once a week and read it front to back. There might even be some business in it in the personals columns."

"Why do I get the feeling you're in charge and not me?

"Cause I am."

"We'll discuss that some other time. In the meantime, can you get me a list of faculty members in the mathematics department? Seems like a good place to start."

"Probably. How soon?"

"Soon as you can."

"OK, but you'll have to hold down the fort while I go to the library. One question."

"Yeah?"

"It's late in the day. Do I get overtime for this?"

"I bought lunch."

"You're buying tomorrow as well."

I walked into my office and looked out the window at a darkening sky. No rain or snow, but the threat was there just waiting to pounce during rush hour. I thought about the case that wasn't a case. Certainly not a paying one at any rate. And other than a personal ethic, I had no obligation to the Dane who got himself plugged in a Manhattan alley. But I was intrigued and since I didn't have anything else on the docket, a few days spent looking into it just to satisfy my own curiosity wouldn't hurt. And there was the nude, of course. I was in love. I went to my desk and pulled a pipe and a pouch of tobacco from the center drawer. After two days without a cigarette, the one I just stubbed out made me dizzier than hell. I was quite surprised at that because I'd been on the Lucky Strike weed for years and didn't think a couple days abstinence would have that much impact. The pipe, because I didn't inhale, wouldn't do that. In addition, it was more satisfying in taste and aroma. Pepper liked it anyway.

Thinking . . . Something was nagging me, some incongruity, something out of place, or in place that I should know or see but it simply escaped me. I shrugged. Maybe I'll dream about it.

I was sitting at my desk filling the pipe and actually looking forward to smoking it when two men walked in, not even pausing at the outer office. They weren't cops. Both were clean shaven and average height but stocky in build and wearing ill-fitting suits. One paused to lean against the wall by the door and the other, who was wearing a dark brown shirt and tan tie, came up to my desk. He reminded me of George Raft in the movie, *Each Dawn I die*, that I'd seen several months before. He was also packing a rod. Like I said, ill-fitting suit and the bulge showed. Without moving my hands, I shifted a bit feeling for my snubnose under my arm. It was just where I'd put it—in the safe. The one in front spoke.

"You are Mr. Grant?"

His English was good but he spoke with an accent. German, I thought, but I'm not all that good with accents. Could be East European.

"I'm Grant."

"I am Mr. Smith and my companion is also Mr. Smith."

I almost laughed, but didn't. My day was just chalk full of Smiths. I set the pipe and tobacco pouch on my desk.

"How can I help you, Mr. Smith?"

"Vee . . . We have learned you are the one who discovered the body of a man in an alley in lower Manhattan. Is that correct?"

"And how did you learn that?"

"The Herald Tribune reported that the body of a Mr. Moller had been discovered by Mr. Grant, a private investigator. Mr. Moller had been shot. Tell me, Mr. Grant, was Mr. Moller alive when you found him?"

"For about thirty seconds."

"Did Mr. Moller say anything?"

"Look, fellas, I went through all this with the Assistant DA. Go ask him. His name is Smith as well. You should get along fine."

The one leaning on the wall pushed himself off and came over to the side of my desk. He still hadn't said anything and kept both hands in his coat pockets. I didn't see a bulge in his coat that would have indicated a gun.

The first Mr. Smith repeated his question. "Did Mr. Moller say anything?"

"No."

"Did he give you anything?"

"No." I wasn't going to give *them* anything either.

"I think you're lying, Mr. Grant."

I didn't even see the other Smith move. I swear it. One second he was standing next to my desk and the next I was sprawled on the floor, the result of a hard smack with his fist on the side of my face just in front of my right ear. At least I think it was his fist. I wasn't quite clear headed at the moment. The same Mr. Smith came around the back of the desk, grabbed two handfuls of my shirt, lifted, and sat me back in my chair. The first Mr. Smith was smiling.

"Now, Mr. Grant, did Mr. Moller say anything or give you anything?"

I'm not a coward but I know when I'm on the losing end of a serious discussion. "No to both questions. When I got to him he was barely alive and bubbling from two holes in the chest and bleeding from the mouth. He mumbled. I couldn't make it out. He died. I hollered for a cop who showed up almost immediately. That's it. That's what I told the cops in the alley and that's what I told the Assistant DA in his office a couple hours ago."

He looked at me for a full minute then nodded to the second Smith who walked back toward the door and took up his old position against the wall.

"I think now you tell the truth."

I didn't say anything but thought, think what you like, you bastard, but don't ever give me a chance to ask the questions.

Without saying another word, he turned and walked out the door with the second Mr. Smith in tow. Forty minutes later I was sitting at my desk holding a cold washcloth to the side of my face when Pepper came back to the office.

"What's wrong with your face?"

"You mean other than ugly?"

"Fall out of your chair?"

"You could say that. Two goons came in here to ask some questions about the shooting in the alley. One got carried away when I wouldn't tell them anything."

"And after they slugged you?"

"It was just the one who popped me on the side of the head. After that, I told them something."

"Like what?"

"Like I lied. I told them the guy died without saying a word and I didn't say anything about the cigarette case."

"Lemme see your face."

I moved the washcloth away and tilted my head to the overhead light.

"Damn, Max, what did the guy hit you with?"

"I thought it was his fist. I didn't see anything in his hand, but I wasn't looking. Could have had a roll of nickels in it."

"Or quarters. You're probably going to be black and blue all the way to the edge of your eye and high on your cheek. You need some ice on it."

"Call the deli and have them send up a quart container of ice. Better add some ham salad and some soup. I have a feeling I won't be able to chew much and I'm not going anywhere tonight."

After she phoned the deli she came back into my office and laid a folder on my desk. "That's a list of math and physics faculty and some general information. Need me for anything else this evening?"

"No, Pepper, I don't. Thank you for everything. Tell Bo I said hi."

"I will. Put the ice on for twenty minutes and then give it a ten minute break. Do that for a couple hours. After that, keeping ice on it won't make much difference. See ya tomorrow."

After she left, I opened the folder and glanced at the couple sheets of notes she'd made. Nothing leaped out at me, but then, nothing was registering very well. She had actually made two lists of faculty, one of the math and physics department and another of a department called the Institute for Advanced Study. Two names at the Institute stood out: Albert Einstein and John von Neumann. AE and JN. I put the file away in my desk drawer and was just standing up when there was a knock at the front door. All I could think of was, ah shit, not again!

But it was just the lad from the deli. I took the package, locked the doors to Pepper's cave and my office, and went to my bedroom. There, I stripped, put on my robe and slippers, and turned on the radio just in time to catch a few minutes of Burns and Allen but switched to a jazz station after laughing at a line by Gracie almost took the side of my head off. I ate with one hand while holding some ice wrapped in a hand towel to my head. After eating, I went to my office, picked up my pipe off my desk and lit it. I couldn't hold it in my mouth but the taste and aroma were grand. To complement the pipe, I fixed myself a stiff bourbon with some leftover ice, went back to my bedroom and after twenty minutes or so, turned off the radio and crawled into bed. Felt good. Slept.

EIGHT

My face felt worse at about six o'clock when I woke, but a look in the mirror showed it wasn't as bad as I expected. There was some redness and an area high on my cheek that looked as though it might turn dark but overall, Pepper's ice seemed to have done the trick.

I completed my morning wake up routine, then walked the few steps to my office. And since I was up earlier than usual, phoned the deli for coffee and Danish. I'd chew slowly. I made up my mind not to be caught un-heeled again, so I strapped on my .38 in the shoulder rig. I also took Pepper's .32 caliber Browning auto from the safe and placed it in my top desk drawer. The Browning doesn't have the punch of the .38 but at ten feet or less, no one cares except the person being shot. While waiting for my coffee, I looked at the couple sheets of paper Pepper had put together the evening before. I became convinced the JN—AE 10 in Moller's notebook referred to a meeting with Albert Einstein and John von Neumann at 10. And it must have been 10 in the morning and not 10 at night because his stamped bus ticket was same day. Ten at night would be too late for a same day bus back to New York.

Thinking of buses, I fished around in the bottom desk drawer and found a bus schedule. There were several daily runs to and from Princeton. Might be worth the trip.

The kid from the deli arrived, and I poured half the large coffee into one of the cups we kept on hand and dunked the Danish in it. We actually had a hotplate, coffee pot, sugar, and some small cans of Carnation condensed milk on hand but we rarely used them since the deli was so convenient. Because it came in a can, Carnation was the butt of jokes and rhymes. One rhyme I remembered had supposedly won a Carnation contest in 1909. The company disavowed it and claimed they had never sponsored a contest, but I thought it so humorous it stuck with me and I mumbled it between bites of soggy Danish.

Carnation Milk is the best in the land.
Here I sit with a can in my hand.
No tits to pull, no hay to pitch,
Just punch a hole in the son of a bitch.

True or not, it was one rhyme that wouldn't make the pages of the Saturday Evening Post or Look magazines. I was still smiling when Pepper came in. She set coffee and donuts on her desk, hung up her coat and babushka, and came into my office.

"You sure look better than I thought you would, boss."

"Feel better, too."

She laid two newspapers on my desk. "The Herald Tribune is from yesterday and there's a short, two paragraph item in it about the guy in the alley, so the thugs who gave you the love tap last night were right. The other paper is today's Times but there's nothing in it about the killing. Might have been yesterday, though."

I glanced at the HT article and Pepper was right. It mentioned the victim's name and mine along with the fact that I was a PI but nothing else. The Smiths from last night could have found my address easy enough in the phone book.

She got her coffee, came back to my desk and sat in the side chair. "Forgot to tell you last evening: we had a call just before you came back from the DA's office from a guy named Bremer who's going through a messy divorce. He needs a PI to look into his wife's activities."

"What did you tell him?"

"Told him you were tied up and to call back about nine o'clock this morning."

"Tell him we realize how important it is to him but we're too busy to handle it. Recommend the Fleming agency."

"Just out of curiosity, Max, how much time do you plan to spend on this?"

I thought about it for a few seconds before answering. "I don't know yet. There's something going on here I don't understand. Call it gut feeling but I think it's deeper and darker that what we see on the surface. In addition, I don't like being slugged by some asshole for something I know little or nothing about."

"Well, right now the case is a freebie and we're not making a dime on it. Our bank account is OK for a few weeks so it's not an immediate problem, but it could get that way after the end of the year. You have any contingency plans?"

"How is it you always ask the right questions at the wrong time?"

"I have a knack for it. Besides, when it comes to money, there is no wrong time. So what's on the agenda for today?"

"You up to a bus ride to Princeton?"

"Sure, if you think it'd be helpful and doesn't include a trip to the battlefield. That wasn't a good experience."

"The sex?"

"No. The rain. I was on top."

"Whoosh!"

"Yeah, that about sums it up. What time do we leave?"

"Take the nine o'clock call from Bremer and then switch the phone over to the answering service. We can catch a bus at ten o'clock."

"OK, boss. Oh, do you think we should call Princeton first to try to make an appointment? I say try because I'd bet it's difficult to get an appointment with just about any faculty member on short notice."

"No, I don't think so. If we tried that, they'd probably put us off till next year if they'd give us one at all. Showing up in person will have a better chance."

I took the cigarette case from my desk, removed the four Camel cigarettes, made sure the folded paper was in place and put the case in my inside suit coat pocket. I debated leaving my handgun in the safe but since I was licensed in New York, New Jersey, and some other nearby states, decided it would be prudent to keep it with me. I put the loose cigarettes in the top desk drawer with Pepper's .32 and locked it.

Bremer phoned at 9:05 and was pissed when Pepper told him we couldn't handle his case but was somewhat mollified when she went on to say what an excellent agency Fleming was and that we often took cases for each other.

The weather was cold but dry and clear with sunshine peeking through some high scattered clouds. The trip to Princeton wasn't a long one, only two stops on the way, and as we got off the bus, I automatically felt in my coat pocket for my cigarettes. What I found was a lump that turned out to be a pipe that I'd filled before we left the office, a medium size bent Kaywoodie. No matter. I suspected a pipe lent itself to the college environment better than cigarettes anyway. I put it between my teeth and lit up.

Pepper smiled. "Except for the hardware you're packing, you might be mistaken for a professor with that pipe in your mouth."

I automatically put my hand over my coat where the snubnose was and asked if it showed.

"Not as long as you don't strip down to your shirt. We'd better ask directions."

Pepper stopped a young fellow carrying some books, and asked where we might find the Institute for Advanced Studies building. We were directed to a large, imposing stone structure just two blocks away. Large trees, bare now in winter, seemed to be scattered randomly on the college grounds and patches of snow could still be seen in building shadows where they lay untouched by sunshine. It was easy to imagine how beautiful the campus would be in summer.

I took a couple puffs on my pipe and turned to Pepper as we walked. "How do you think we should play this?"

"Hell, boss, it's your show. I'm just along for the ride and some bad memories, but since you ask, was there someone in particular you want to see?"

"I have a gut feeling the initials JN and AE in Hans Moller's notebook refer to John von Neumann and Albert Einstein. I'd like to see either of them."

"Well, since you're not FDR or the president of the university, I suspect you have little chance of seeing either, particularly since you have no appointment—not that you were likely to get one anyway. But since we're here, we can ask."

We entered the building and walked to the information desk located to the right side of the entrance. It was manned by a bespectacled young fellow reading a text book.

"May I help you?"

"My name is Max Grant and this is my associate, Paula Brown. We'd like to see Albert Einstein or John von Neumann, please."

A flicker of a smile crossed the young lad's face. "I take it you don't have an appointment with either professor?"

"No, but we've come from New York on the outside chance they might be available. It's a matter of some importance."

"A phone call would have saved you time and trouble. As it happens, they're both in New York attending a conference, a closed conference with other physicists and mathematicians. I often work as an assistant to both professors. Is there something I can help you with?"

I replied, "No, no thank you, but could you tell us where their meeting is in New York?"

"No, I'm afraid not."

His reply sounded more wouldn't than couldn't. We turned away as he bent his head back over his text book. We walked several steps when intuition took over. I turned back and said, "Yes, perhaps you can help. Has a Mr. Hans Moller been here to see either professor?"

His head snapped up so fast his glasses bounced once on his nose. He stuttered. "D-d-did you know Mr. Moller?"

I stepped back to the desk, leaned forward over it, and growled. "Your use of past tense shows you know Moller is dead and your reaction tells me he was here. So, did he meet with either professor?"

"N-n-no, they had already gone to New York. He met with Professor Emit Fielding, an assistant to Professor von Neumann. Did you know Mr. Moller?" His stutter was fading away.

"No. I found him in an alley shot twice in the chest. Bubbling. Blood all over. He died in thirty seconds."

The poor boy's face had gone white and was fast shading to green. I thought he was going to up-chuck his cookies on the desk. I was snarling outside, grinning inside. Pepper had turned to face the door, trying to hide a smile.

My growl was in rare form. "We'd like to speak with Professor Fielding. Now!"

"Yes sir. I'll see if he's in, sir."

He picked up the phone, dialed a three digit number, and waited about five seconds. "This is Mike at the front desk. There's a gentleman and his associate here who would like to meet with you, sir." Pause. "Yes, sir, I understand, sir, but it's about Mr. Moller." Pause. "Thank you."

There was a sigh of relief behind the "Thank you."

Without stuttering he said, "If you'll wait in the alcove over there—" He pointed to a grotto like area about thirty feet away that held several overstuffed chairs and a low table. "Professor Fielding will be with you in a few minutes."

We didn't bother to sit down. Just as well. Fielding showed up in about three minutes. His appearance looked typical professor to me: about five-eight, late fifties or early sixties, thinning light brown hair, neatly trimmed beard, and a slight stoop. He was wearing a tan tweed jacket and brown pants, all baggy, and carrying a thin leather briefcase that he sat on the table before he turned to me.

No preamble, handshake or niceties. "And you are?"

He pissed me off. "Nice to meet you too." I turned to Pepper. "Come on, let's go back to New York and let this jerk stew in his own shit."

"No—no! Wait! I'm sorry. I'm a bit on edge. Mike said you knew Mr. Moller and we just learned yesterday evening that he'd been murdered after visiting here." He put out his hand. "My name is Fielding."

We shook hands. "Max Grant. This is my associate, Paula Brown."

"Please have a seat."

We did. Opposite Fielding and across the table. He sat, then leaned forward.

"Were you a friend of Mr. Moller's?"

"No. I'm a private investigator. I found him as he was dying."

Fielding winced and paused a few seconds before asking, "I assume you have spoken with the police, but if you didn't know Mr. Moller, why are you here?"

The guy was a quick thinker. Analytical. But then, I assumed those traits came with the territory.

"Information provided by the police and some additional inquiries by Miss Brown led us to Princeton. Moller sensed he was dying and with the breath he had left, asked me to do something."

"And that was?"

I took the case from my pocket and handed it to him. "To find the nude on the cigarette case."

He was looking at me as he took the case but when his eyes dropped, his mouth came open and he actually stopped breathing for a few seconds. I didn't think it was because he had never seen a nude before.

I pointed to the case. "Do you know her? Or more to the point, do you know Sarah Bennett?" The stuttering syndrome had moved from the reception desk to the alcove.

"W-w-well . . . . I-I . . ."

I reached to retrieve the case and he pulled back. "Look, professor, you met with Moller and it's pretty obvious you know Sarah Bennett. I'm just a PI trying to do what I was asked to do by a dying man, in addition to finding out about some information that piqued my interest."

"What information?" Surprise. Stutter gone.

"Open the case."

He opened the case, removed the paper, unfolded it and pressed it out flat on the table. He ran his index finger over each line as he read. When he finished, he looked at me. "This was in the case Moller gave to you?"

"Yes, folded, just like you found it." I didn't tell him I'd removed the cigarette case from Moller's pocket after he'd pawed his coat. In a sense, Moller did give it to me.

Pepper chimed in. "It's obviously nuclear related. Hypothetical. Or is it?"

Fielding was still looking at the paper and mumbled, "Yes . . . partially hypothetical . . ." His head snapped up and he looked at Pepper. "You are a scientist?"

Pepper smiled. "No, physics wasn't my major, but it doesn't take a scientist to figure out the document is referring to something atomic. Also, it's incomplete."

"Incomplete?"

"What's the last word on the page?"

"*By* is the last word. Ahh . . . I see. An additional page or pages follow."

"Yes, and on the other side of the paper is something hand written with a few additional equations below."

Fielding turned it over. "Hvis vi antager. It's Danish and mine is rusty but I think it translates to, 'If we assume.' But what follows doesn't appear to be of any value, just a common physics formula, and the rest of the page is blank. It could be a note to himself, not related to the front of the page. Moller was Danish but I don't believe he was a scientist."

I started to reach for my pipe but thought better of it and simply looked at Fielding. "From your reaction, I take it you've not seen this paper before."

"No, I have not."

"But I suspect Moller had it with him when you met. I wonder why he didn't show it to you."

The professor folded the paper, put it back in the case, closed it, then sat back in his chair with his head down. We waited. It was a full minute before he raised his head and began to speak.

"I didn't give Moller much of a chance. He was aggressive. He claimed to have an appointment with Professor Einstein or von Neumann but we had no record of it, and in any case, they were unavailable. He wanted to know if Miss Bennett was here on campus. I told him no. He asked if I knew where she was. I told him no. He insisted I must know but I told him I couldn't help him and walked away. He left. I must say that in spite of his Danish nationality, intuition tells me he may be working for the Nazis." He half smiled. "Or if demeanor is any indication, maybe he should be." He paused again as if deciding what to say next.

Decision made, he went on. "Sarah Bennett is no longer a member of the Princeton faculty but has a close relationship with some members of the Institute for Advanced Study. She is a mathematician and very knowledgeable in physics. She is also a noted art dealer and in that capacity, travels to the art centers of many European countries, most notably France, England, Norway, Denmark and Holland. While in those countries, she would of course have opportunities to meet informally with members of their scientific community, perhaps at a dinner or an art museum. And what would be discussed might not always relate to art."

This time I did take my pipe from my pocket and lit it. "In other words, she's a spy."

"No, not in the sense you mean. She doesn't work for the government, but instead, she facilitates the transfer of crucial information between members of the scientific community who share a common interest in opposing the domination of Europe, perhaps the world, by Hitler." He paused again but this time only to reach into his jacket pocket for his own pipe and pouch of tobacco. We waited till he filled the pipe and lit it.

After several puffs, he continued. "What I'm about to say is not really secret though it is not widely known by the public either. But I share it with you only because I believe we must find Miss Bennett. She may be in receipt of important information, either in writing or in her head. She was to have returned to this country several days ago and meet with Professor von Neumann but no one has seen her.

"It's common knowledge among the scientific community in this country, England, and several other countries that credible work is being done in the area of nuclear fission. Papers have been published in scientific journals and information shared among physicists. These papers are a matter of public record. It is widely believed that a weapon, perhaps a bomb, of unimaginable force could be developed, but that belief is not well known, at least among the general public. There is, however, a great fear that if such a device could be built, it might be done by Germany, with catastrophic results for the rest of the world. We do know that in September of this year, a research group was formed in Germany with the express purpose of examining the possibilities and implications of nuclear fission. So far, no comparable research group has been formed here.

"Now, Mr. Grant, I have a question for you. Do you think you can find Miss Bennett? And being a practical man, I must ask what the expenses will be if you care to undertake such a task."

I didn't tell him I intended to look for Sarah Bennett in any case. "My fee is twenty-five dollars per day plus expenses, with less than a day prorated. And that's for my agency. There's no charge per operative." Pepper raised an eyebrow at that statement. We only had one operative. Me. "We require a one hundred dollar retainer but that is applied toward the fee. If we should find her in two days, for example, you would receive a refund of fifty dollars, less expenses. But knowing what I know, I think it unlikely we'll find her in just a few days. Any information, any background you can give us would be helpful."

"I'll have a check in the mail to you today. How should it be made out?"

"Grant Agency. I'll sign and send you two copies of the contract. Sign one copy and return it. Keep the other for your file."

Fielding tamped and relit his pipe. "Well, you know what Miss Bennett looks like. Though the photo is several years old, she's changed little. She's about five feet five with chestnut colored hair. She was to have sailed aboard the French liner De Grasse from Le Havre to New York, scheduled to arrive three days ago and meet with Professor Neumann a day later. She didn't. We waited a day and then did some quiet checking. That was yesterday. She was on the passenger list but when we checked the hotel she usually frequents when in New York, we found she had a reservation but had not checked in. Thinking she may have had an accident or had become ill, my assistant phoned all the local hospitals but they had no record she'd been admitted."

"Where was her hotel reservation?"

"The Savoy-Plaza at Central Park."

"Expensive."

"Aside from art, nice hotels were her only extravagance. She dealt in art on a small scale but I daresay it provided her with more than a decent income, certainly better than an assistant professorship at a university or college."

"Alright, just between us, do you have any ideas or suspicions?"

"I know it's a cliché but I suspect foul play. Perhaps she was waylaid and is being held somewhere. I only hope no harm has come to her."

"Have you considered notifying the police that she's missing?"

"I thought about it but by what authority? She's not an employee of the college in the normal sense and we are not family. So far as I know, she has no family, or at least I've never heard her speak of any. To go to the police and say she might be carrying crucial scientific information would undoubtedly require an explanation. And it's entirely possible that the police, wishing to pass the buck, would notify federal authorities. Notifying the FBI or some other government agency might not be a bad idea but their intervention might seriously disrupt the college. Your interest in her disappearance, accidental as it may be, is a godsend."

My pipe had gone out so I simply slid it back into my jacket pocket. "It's possible she's in hiding for some reason, afraid to contact anyone here. Did she have any friends outside the academic community?"

"She dated a lab assistant here but I don't think they've seen each other for more than a year. His name is Larry Spence. The only other person I know of is a girlfriend of hers she would visit museums with. They'd occasionally have dinner when she was in town. Her name is Ariella Blumfeld.

"Jewish." I made it a statement, not a question.

"Yes, I believe so."

"Do you know where she lives?"

"Brooklyn. Brownsville, or perhaps, Canarsie."

As I took the case back from Fielding, I said, "Thank you. At least it's a starting point." I stood—Pepper did the same. "Give me your phone number and we'll call you in a couple days. Sooner if we learn anything important."

It was about one in the afternoon when we left the administration building to walk to the bus terminal. The sky had become gray and overcast with a promise of snow. I'm not a superstitious fellow but the seemed to be an omen. We had little to go on in the hunt for Sarah Bennett.

NINE

When we arrived at our office, I put the case in the safe, asked Pepper to call the deli for a couple sandwiches and to check the answering service for any calls while we were gone. A few minutes later she was in my office with a notepad in her hand.

"We had two calls while we were out, one from Mr. Bremer thanking us for suggesting the Fleming agency, and the second from the DA's office asking you to call."

My mind was elsewhere and it was twenty seconds before I replied. "Nice of Bremer to call but we've probably lost a future client. Ah well, can't be helped. I'll call DA Smith Monday. He'll be pissed about something whether I call today or never, so I may as well put it off. Tell you what, when the sandwiches arrive, let's sit in here and talk about my nude."

She turned, started to walk out, but turned back. "You really have a thing about her, don't you?"

I waited a bit before replying. Thinking . . . "I make jokes about being in love with her and admit I was drawn to her the minute I saw her picture. It wasn't that she was nude. Hell, I've seen plenty of nudes in my time, most in the flesh. It was something else, something I'm not sure I can put into words. Maybe if there is such a thing as Damsel in Distress Syndrome, I have it."

"Ya know, Max, I think it may be more than that." She smiled. "I'm going to go powder my nose, and no, you can't hold my leg."

I laughed. I needed the laugh.

While Pepper was gone, I dug into my stash cabinet thinking I'd have a cigarette. Instead, I lifted out an unsmoked pipe I'd bought a couple weeks before at Jake Resnik's suggestion. It was a Sasieni, made in England, which I thought odd. A name like Sasieni just didn't seem British. But it was stamped *Made In England* in kind of a football shape, and even had a patent number that Jake said was stamped on pipes exported to the States. It was also stamped Hurlingham, which did sound British to me, and was what I would call chubby, with a thick, slightly rounded bowl that had a gnarled finish. It was straight, with a tapered stem that had four small light blue dots on the side. The thought of trying out a new pipe completely banished the desire for a cigarette so I filled it about three-quarters full and went back to my desk. I was enjoying the first few puffs on my pipe when Pepper returned and sat in the chair in front of my desk.

"You want to talk now or wait for lunch? Late lunch, I might add. I had visions of a nice restaurant after the trip to Princeton but instead we get delivered deli and Cokes."

"Well, you're the one always complaining about the state of our bank account. I'm just trying to live up to your high standards."

She laughed. "Boss, you're a lying sack of shit. You're just saving a few bucks so you can drop it on the bar at Jimmy's."

"You're picking on me again," I said, smiling. "I'm going to have to talk to Bo about teaching you a little respect."

"Bo would be teaching you. He thinks I walk on water. Speaking of which, we saw an ad for a hydrostatic bed, a mattress filled with water. Bo said he'd like to try it. I told him it might add to the action, but we'd both get seasick."

I didn't say anything, just looked at her.

"What?"

"Nothing. I'm just trying to picture the action."

"You have no idea, boss. In your wildest dreams—"

There was a tap at the front door and the lad from the deli came in, set a brown bag and a couple Cokes on Peppers desk, waved, and left. Pepper got up and brought lunch to my desk.

I set my pipe in the ashtray. "What'd you order for me?"

"A shit sandwich. What do you always order?"

"Ham and swiss on rye."

"Well, today ain't no different."

"What'd you get for yourself?"

"Same. You want to compare sizes?

"No way I'm going to touch that question."

"Alright," she said, as she sat and unwrapped her sandwich, "Let's talk nude."

I let that comment go as well and opened both Cokes. "What I want to do is start from the beginning and run through what we know. You stop me any time with questions or comments."

"Sounds good. Go ahead."

"I left Jimmy's and was crossing the alleyway about a hundred feet south of the bar when I heard two shots. They were muffled like they'd been fired through a coat or from a gun with a silencer, though it could have simply been the rain and snow that cut down on the sound. If it was with a silencer, the gun couldn't have been an automatic because the shots, though muffled, were too loud, so it must have been a revolver which can't be silenced as much as an automatic. We'll probably never know so it doesn't make much difference. I pulled my .38 snub from my rig, held it in my pocket, and went into the alley."

She held up her finger and finished chewing. "How fast did you move into the alley? See anything out of the ordinary?"

"I moved slowly, and believe me, I was looking. Had no desire to get shot, but at the time, I still didn't know the pile laying there was a body. When I got to the guy, who I later found out was Hans Moller, he was pawing his coat and mumbling to find the nude on the cigarette case. I hollered for a cop, then fished in his inside coat pocket and found the case. One cop showed up and then went off for the precinct sergeant and that's when I took a quick look at the case. All that was in it was four Camel cigarettes and the folded paper. I didn't get a good look till after I came back here. The following day, I talked with Jake Resnik and he sent me to Rubin Stein where I got the additional photos and learned her name was Sarah Bennett. Then I later visited Assistant DA Smith and learned a bit more."

"Like what? I mean, you told me some when you returned from Smith's office but were too pissed at Smith to go into detail. Go over it again."

"I learned the dead guy's name; that he was carrying fifty bucks and some Danish money, a small notebook with JA—AE 10 and Sarah Bennett's name written in it. He also had a comb, handkerchief, change, a Swiss army knife, and a half pack of Chesterfield cigarettes."

She took a sip of her Coke. "Chesterfield cigarettes?"

"Yeah, why?"

"If he smoked Chesterfields, why did he have Camels in the case?"

"Son of a bitch! That's what's been nagging me. I knew I was missing something. I don't know why it was Camels instead of Chesterfields. Maybe something as simple as sampling different brands while here in the States."

"Or maybe they belong to someone else. Where are they?"

"Here, in the desk drawer." I opened the drawer and set the four cigarettes on the desk between us. "They look normal. Tobacco's a bit loose, but they're stale and dry so that's not unusual."

Pepper picked them up one by one and looked closely at them. "Two of them have a very tiny dot in the C of Camel, but the ones without the dot seem heavier. Take a look."

I did and she was right. "The two without the dot do seem slightly heavier. I think maybe we should do a bit of surgery."

I took a small razor knife from my desk drawer and very carefully sliced one of the non-dot cigarettes from end to end and peeled the paper back. In the center, rolled tightly, was a piece of paper. Using a fingernail and the knife blade, I unrolled it. It was thin, onion skin, about an inch and a half in width and four inches long unrolled, with something printed on it in very small letters. I found a magnifying glass in my top desk drawer and looked at the paper. In the upper right hand corner there was a 1/2 but most of the rest of it, though in English, was meaningless to me. There was something about the use of heavy water or graphite but beyond that, I was out of my league. I passed the glass to Pepper and she studied it for a couple minutes while I finished off my sandwich.

She set the magnifying glass down on my desk. “Doesn’t make much sense to me and probably not to you either. The 1/2 may mean first sheet of two but that’s a guess. Let’s open the other cigarette.”

We did and in the upper right hand corner was a 2/2. The rest of it was as incomprehensible as the first sheet. I sat back in my chair, put my hands behind my head and looked at Pepper.

“Well, educated one, what do you think?”

“I think we have two sheets of something important. Someone else could have more.”

“My nude?”

“Good guess.”

“And she’s missing. This information might be the reason why.”

She picked up her Coke and took a sip. “What do you think? Should we turn these over to Professor Fielding?”

“That’s one option.”

"Is there another?"

"Yeah . . . maybe. They could be used as a bargaining chip. Or for that matter, we could use the folded paper in the cigarette case."

"For Sarah Bennett?"

"For Bennett or more information if we need it."

"Information from who? . . . Or is that whom?"

"Who cares? Maybe two guys named Smith."

Pepper set her empty Coke in the wooden rack. It held 24 empties and when it was full, the boy from the deli took them back. "How you going to find them?"

"They found me, remember?"

"Yeah, but they had a reason named Moller. They must have believed your story or they'd have been back. I suppose you could advertise."

"That's what I was thinking."

"You're kidding!"

"No, I think it's a sparkling idea and we know they read the newspapers, but I think I'll hold off for a couple days. I want to check out some other things first."

She chuckled. "Well, boss, if you do put an ad in the newspaper, you want me to ask Bo to move in here for a few days?"

"Might not be a bad idea. I'll let you know."

I sent Pepper home, hit my stash cabinet for some bourbon, lit my pipe and sat at my desk thinking, an exercise that hasn't always been my strong point. I rely more on intuition, gut feeling, than analysis but maybe the analysis goes on subconsciously. My decisions and solutions seem to be right much more often than not. So . . . start at the beginning, and the beginning wasn't when Moller got shot in the alley, it was when Sarah Bennett got off the ship.

Intuition kicked in. I opened the top desk drawer, pulled out my address book, thumbed through to the M's, picked up the phone and dialed. He picked up on the third ring.

"Hello?"

"Murphy?"

"Yeah?"

"Max Grant. Tomorrow is Saturday. You off?"

"Aye, lad, that I am."

"I have a job for you. It involves some walking. You up to that?"

"I'd love it. Be like old times on a beat."

"Alright. Be here at my office at ten o'clock tomorrow morning."

"Count on it."

"Thanks, Murph. See ya tomorrow."

I considered going for a walk, hit a local bar for a drink or two, and maybe connect with a companion for the evening but one look out the window put an end to that. Rain mixed with snow. Dismal and dark.

Instead, I went to my stash cabinet, poured myself two more fingers of bourbon, went back to my desk and picked up the Sasieni pipe I'd smoked earlier. I tamped down the ash and then looked over the books on the shelf below the cabinet. I had some good ones including Doyle, Steinbeck and Hemingway but wasn't in the mood for something heavy. Instead, I chose a thin collection of short stories by Mark Twain that included *Extracts from Adam's Diary*. I had started to read it several weeks before and found it humorous enough that I several times chuckled out loud.

Gathering up book, bourbon, and pipe, I checked to be sure the office doors were locked and went to my bedroom. I was soon in my robe, in my chair, and found a radio station featuring Duke Ellington and his band. Bourbon at hand, pipe lit, book on lap. I was tired. Bedtime in two hours if I could make it that long. I didn't.

TEN

Saturday morning. It was a damp winter cold that had settled over Princeton through the night, and walking up Washington Road on the university campus, Professor Emit Fielding was chilled through. He felt it more in his back than anywhere but his breathing was a bit labored as well. Could be another bout of pneumonia coming on, he thought, or maybe my age is just catching up with me.

John von Neumann had returned from his New York meeting the previous evening but without Albert Einstein. Einstein had chosen to spend the weekend in Manhattan with friends. Von Neumann phoned Fielding to ask about Sarah Bennett and when told she was still missing, asked if anything was being done to find her—the police for instance. When Fielding told him something was being done but he would prefer to discuss it in person, von Neumann suggested they meet in one of the conversation rooms on the third floor of Fine Hall at ten o'clock the following morning.

Fine Hall had been the home of the Department of Mathematics of the Institute for Advanced Study for almost six years, during which time a new facility, Fuld Hall, was built and dedicated completely to the Institute. By late 1939, most of the professors and researchers had moved to the new facility but some still preferred to use the library located on the third floor of Fine Hall. Fielding was one of them as was von

Neumann but that would gradually change as the library at Fuld was built up.

Fielding often smiled when he thought of the Fine Hall library. The reason was the librarian, Margaret Shields, a small but energetic woman affectionately known as “Bunny” for her size. She was gifted in mathematics and physics and with a remarkable memory. A grad student or professor would ask her, “Do you remember that paper on atomic structure by Niels Bohr I was reviewing several days ago?” and she'd reply, “Of course. One moment and I'll get it for you.” And she would. Whether it was memory or prescience no one knew or cared. Bunny Shields was a gem.

Fielding turned left at the walkway that went past the Palmer Physical Laboratory and then right to walk between the Laboratory and Fine Hall. He went in the side door of Fine and then to the lobby where he took the elevator to the third floor. He could have walked up the stairs but simply didn't feel up to it. There was a grad student at the library desk and Fielding asked if von Neumann had come in yet. He was told, yes, Professor von Neumann was in the northwest conversation room.

When Fielding entered the room, von Neumann was sitting in an overstuffed chair with some papers spread out in front of him on a coffee table. He nodded and Fielding moved a smaller chair to the opposite side of the coffee table and sat down. It felt good to sit. He could have just closed his eyes and . . .

“Good morning, Emit. You look tired. Did you not sleep well?”

"Slept alright, John, but feel as if I'm coming down with a cold or flu."

"Perhaps you should stop by the dispensary later. Have them look at you."

"I think I will. I had a bout with pneumonia last year. Don't want another. How was your meeting in New York?"

"Good, good—a lively discussion. Teller and Wigner were there, and of course, Leo Szilard who, with Einstein, wrote a letter to Roosevelt in August pointing out the danger that would arise if Germany developed the first atomic bomb. Roosevelt's response came back just a few weeks ago at the end of October. In it, he noted the establishment of a committee composed of Army and Navy staff and headed by Alexander Sachs to study uranium and the feasibility of a uranium bomb.

"We know the Germans have formed a group called *Uranverein*, and at least three of the members, Walther Gerlach, Erich Schumann, and Kurt Diebner, are prominent mathematicians or physicists, but I think Werner Heisenberg may be involved as well. What we don't know is how far along they are with their research and how wide a net they've thrown to bring other scientists into their group. We were hoping Sarah Bennett or Hans Moller might be able to provide some of that information."

Fielding brought his pipe out of his coat pocket and held it in his hand, but didn't make any move to light it. "Moller is dead."

Von Neumann's head snapped up. "When?"

"The day you left for New York. It was in the newspapers but just a paragraph. I thought perhaps you'd seen it."

"No. No I haven't. Accident?"

"Murdered. Shot down in an alley in Lower Manhattan. Interestingly, he was found by a private investigator named Max Grant who was walking past the alley and heard the shots. Moller lived long enough to tell Mr. Grant to find the nude on the cigarette case."

"Cigarette case?"

"Yes. It seems Mr. Grant got the case from Moller. It was an old case with a picture of Sarah Bennett on the front, nude from the waist up. In it was a folded sheet of paper with nuclear related information on it. Mr. Grant chose not to share the case with the police."

"You talk as though you've seen the paper."

"I have. Mr. Grant and his associate brought it here along with the case."

"Quit fiddling with your pipe, Emit, and light it. Your tobacco has a very nice aroma. You say Mr. Grant brought the paper here? How did he know to come here?"

"As I said, he's an investigator. He managed to cobble together enough information to lead him here. His associate is an attractive Negro woman who impresses me as better educated than Mr. Grant, but he's determined and tenacious. I've asked him to look into the disappearance of Sarah Bennett though I got the impression he intended to do that anyway."

"And why would he do that?"

"I think he was enamored by the picture of Sarah Bennett."

Von Neumann smiled. "You hired him?"

"Yes. It's a minor expense and I suspect his chances of finding her may be better than the police who have other things of greater importance on their plate than looking for a missing person."

Von Neumann sat back in his chair and smiled again. "Sarah Bennett nude, huh?"

"From the waist up." Fielding was also smiling.

"I wonder why."

"She appeared young, perhaps early twenties. She may have needed the money to go to school."

"What does this Mr. Grant look like?"

"Just under six feet, brown hair with heavy mustache, maybe mid-thirties. Ruggedly handsome."

Von Neumann laughed. "Maybe he's in love with Miss Bennett, or at least, with the Miss Bennett on the cigarette case."

"Maybe. I didn't get that impression from our conversation but it does seem likely."

"Did you get the paper that was in the case?"

"No. He took it with him but it was preamble to more detail. I suspect Miss Bennett has the same or possibly related information she gathered while in Europe. It surprises me Moller didn't have more."

"He may have but perhaps it hasn't been found yet. We must find Bennett. I have to tell you, Emit, this endeavor to investigate the feasibility of making an atomic bomb is serious, quite serious. Our way of life may depend upon it. Hitler is on the move in Europe with the most powerful war machine seen this century. If his people succeed in making an atomic bomb first, he may rule the world. We can't let that happen."

"Do you really believe it could happen?"

"I do. Remember—Einstein wrote to Roosevelt in August and it was almost three months before he received a reply and that reply appeared lukewarm as regards any firm commitment. And typical of a bureaucrat, Roosevelt asked Alexander Sachs to form a committee. I'm not saying nothing will come of it but I'm concerned we won't act as quickly as we should. Have you seen the letters?"

No, I'm afraid I haven't."

Von Neumann opened a folder that was lying on the table and passed two papers to Fielding. "These are photographic copies. Read them and tell me if you agree with me."

Fielding picked up the first, by Einstein, and read.

Albert Einstein
Old Grove Road
Peconic, Long Island
August 2nd, 1939

F.D. Roosevelt
President of the United States
White House
Washington, D.C.

Sir:

Some recent work by E. Fermi and L. Szilard, which has been communicated to me in manuscript, leads me to expect that the element uranium may be turned into a new and important source of energy in the immediate future. Certain aspects of the situation which has arisen seem to call for watchfulness and if necessary, quick action on the part of the

Administration. I believe therefore that it is my duty to bring to your attention the following facts and recommendations.

In the course of the last four months it has been made probable through the work of Joliot in France as well as Fermi and Szilard in America—that it may be possible to set up a nuclear chain reaction in a large mass of uranium, by which vast amounts of power and large quantities of new radium-like elements would be generated. Now it appears almost certain that this could be achieved in the immediate future.

This new phenomenon would also lead to the construction of bombs, and it is conceivable—though much less certain—that extremely powerful bombs of this type may thus be constructed. A single bomb of this type, carried by boat and exploded in a port, might very well destroy the whole port together with some of the surrounding territory. However, such bombs might very well prove too heavy for transportion by air.

The United States has only very poor ores of uranium in moderate quantities. There is some good ore in Canada and former Czechoslovakia, while the most important source of uranium is in the Belgian Congo.

In view of this situation you may think it desirable to have some permanent contact maintained between the Administration and the group of physicists working on chain reactions in America. One possible way of achieving this might be for you to entrust the task with a person who has your confidence and who could perhaps serve in an unofficial capacity. His task might comprise the following:

a) to approach Government Departments, keep them informed of the further development, and put forward recommendations for Government action, giving particular attention to the problem of securing a supply of uranium ore for the United States.
b) to speed up the experimental work, which is at present being carried on within the limits of the budgets of University laboratories, by providing funds, if such funds be required, through his contacts with private persons who are willing to make contributions for this cause, and perhaps also by obtaining co-operation of industrial laboratories which have necessary equipment.

I understand that Germany has actually stopped the sale of uranium from the Czechoslovakian mines which she has taken over. That she should have taken such early action might perhaps be understood on the ground that the son of the German Under-Secretary of State, von Weizsacker, is attached to the Kaiser-Wilhelm Institute in Berlin, where some of the American work on uranium is now being repeated.

Yours very truly,

A. Einstein

Albert Einstein

Fielding set the Einstein letter down and picked up Roosevelt's reply. "Professor Einstein was certainly specific enough and his final paragraph should prompt some timely action on the part of the government."

"One would certainly think so," said Von Neumann, "but read the reply."

THE WHITE HOUSE
WASHINGTON

October 19, 1939

My dear Professor:

I want to thank you for your recent letter and the most interesting and important enclosure.

I found this data of such import that I have convened a Board consisting of the head of the Bureau of Standards and a chosen representative of the Army and Navy to thoroughly investigate the possibilities of your suggestion regarding the element of uranium.

I am glad to say that Dr. Sachs will cooperate and work with this Committee and I feel this is the most practical and effective method of dealing with the subject.

Please accept my sincere thanks.

Dr. Albert Einstein,
Old Grove Road,
Nassau Point,
Poconic, Long Island,
New York

Fielding set the Roosevelt letter on top of Einstein's and slid them back to von Neumann "Not exactly an enthusiastic reply, is it?"

"No, and that concerns me. Deeply. Well Emit, I must be going. I think you should walk over to the dispensary before going home. Whether you are coming down with flu, pneumonia, or simply a bad cold, they should be able to give you something to help."

"I'll do that as soon as I leave here and then I think I'll go home, fix myself a hot toddy and go to bed for the remainder of the weekend. If there are additional exchanges between Einstein, or anyone here, and the government, I'd appreciate it if you'd keep me informed. And I'll do the same if I hear anything from Mr. Grant or his associate about Miss Bennett."

ELEVEN

Saturday mornings are usually lazy for me unless I'm working on a case that involves weekends. Divorce cases are like that. Husbands will claim they're going to the golf course or gym and wives will claim shopping, but a half hour after leaving home they may both be knocking off a piece in a hotel room or someone else's place. And that's where yours truly, armed with camera and tape recorder, earns enough to keep my stash cabinet stocked and pay Pepper a decent wage.

I woke early but still took my time. No rush. Murphy wasn't due till ten. About nine o'clock, the kid from the deli delivered my usual morning breakfast and picked up the envelope with the cash that paid for the regular deliveries. As usual, I included a nice tip for the lad. Sunday was the only day I laid in something for myself or went out to one of the local diners.

At five minutes till ten—I had just finished looking at a section of the New York City map that included the dock area for liner arrivals and departures—there was a tap at the door.

"Come in, Murph, door's open."

"Morning, Max."

"Still rain and snow outside? I haven't looked."

"Snow, but light. An inch on the ground, if that."

I picked up my pipe and lit it. "Still feel like some walking? Not all will be outside, but enough."

"I'm wearing my galoshes. At least my feet will be dry. Where am I headed and what am I looking for?"

Shifting the map around so we could both see it, I said, "To the dock area. Arrivals and departures. You'll be trying to get a line on a passenger who arrived four days ago on the French liner De Grasse from Le Havre. A woman named Sarah Bennett. About five-feet-five, brown hair, slender. I don't know what color eyes. Talk to porters or anyone else you think may have seen her, including drivers at the taxi stand. You might want to wander for several blocks in each direction to see if anyone saw her walking or in a cab."

I went to the floor safe and brought out the cigarette case. "This is who you're looking for, Murph."

"Oh, wow! I'm in love. And at my age . . ."

"Shut up, Murph. That's my line."

"Why am I looking for her, Max? I don't need to know but an old man gets curious."

I paused and took a few seconds to relight my pipe. "For now, let's just say I'm in love. I think she's being held by some bad guys and I want to find her. You may get some helpful information but I don't think you'll locate her. If by chance you do, don't do anything to get yourself spotted. Get the hell away and phone me as soon as you can. If I'm not here, leave a message with the answering service. You packing?"

"Yeah, my .38 service revolver in my overcoat pocket."

"One other thing. Don't flash your badge unless you think it will buy you something worthwhile. I'd just as soon whoever is holding her doesn't know we're looking."

"Okay, Max. You want me to come back here or just call?"

"Call is fine. And don't wear yourself out. Four hours is probably enough to cover the area. Just let me know the time you put in and I'll pay you the standard operative rate. Good enough?"

"Fine, Lad. And Max? Thanks for putting an old man back in harness again. I appreciate it."

I smiled. "Hell, Murph, I'm just lazy. I'm getting a good, experienced cop to do my legwork for me."

After Murphy left, I decided I'd better do a bit of legwork myself. Professor Fielding mentioned a woman friend of Sarah Bennett's named Ariella Blumfeld who lived somewhere in Brooklyn, probably the Brownsville area. I checked the phone book. No A or Ariella Blumfeld but there were seven Blumfelds listed. I decided to call them all on the off chance she was married or living with family. I hit it on number five listed as GA Blumfeld.

"Hello."

"Hello, I'm calling for an Ariella Blumfeld."

"I am Ariella. Who are you?" She had a slight accent. German, I thought.

"My name is Max Grant."

"Should I know you Mr. Grant?"

"No you shouldn't, but I'm trying to locate Sarah Bennett."

Long pause.

"Hello. Are you still there?"

"Yes. Why are you looking for Sarah?"

"Because she's missing. She was supposed to meet with some professors at Princeton University several days ago but didn't arrive. I'm a private investigator and they asked me to look into it. May I come see you?"

Another pause. Shorter.

"Yes, but not before noon."

"Noon is fine. Is the address in the phone book correct?"

"Yes. It's on Hinsdale between Dumont and Blake. Apartment 2B."

"I'll find it. Thank you."

It meant a bus ride to 98th and Dumont and a trolley to Hinsdale. Not all that far but because I had no idea what Saturday schedules were and it was going on eleven, I decided I'd leave now. I went into my bedroom and slipped on my shoulder rig with my .38 in it and put my jacket on. I considered whether to take the cigarette case with me. Decided against it. I did stop at my stash cabinet and debated pocketing the half pack of Lucky Strikes lying on the shelf, but instead took out a fresh pipe and a pouch of Edgeworth tobacco. My wool newsboy cap and scarf went on before my overcoat and I paused to look around the office to see if I was forgetting anything. Nope.

It had stopped snowing. I walked out the front door of the building, stopped, lit my pipe, and savored the flavor and aroma of the tobacco as I never have a cigarette. Must be the weather. It was misty, and the air was crisp. It reminded me of winter mornings as a child in

Amherst, just outside Buffalo in upstate New York. I was fourteen and had a paper route. Not many customers, just 35, but I saved up enough to buy a bike. A Schwinn. Less than a month later someone stole it. I never found out who, and never saw it again. Didn't buy another bike either but that's when I decided to become a cop. Well, we all make mistakes.

My mistake was in thinking the courts were too slow in dispensing justice in certain circumstances and I appointed myself to that esteemed office. There were situations when Precinct Captains looked the other way, and occasionally, I took advantage of it. I was a beat cop on the lower east side, working the night shift, when a young woman came running out of a tenement screaming that her boyfriend was beating their three month old baby. I stormed into the room just as he was raising his hand over the child who was in a crib, screaming and crying. He stopped, put both his hands up and said, "Whoa." I took it to mean he was resisting arrest. That's what I told the sergeant, anyway. The ambulance attendant said he had broken ribs, broken nose, his right ear hanging on by a thread and various other contusions and lacerations. Those wooden tire thumpers we carried were deadly.

That one was overlooked. The one that got me in real trouble was when I stepped in between a man and his wife who were fighting outside a nightclub. Well, he was throwing punches and she was the bag. I watched while he hit her twice with his fist. She went down the second time. When she got up, he raised his fist for a third time. I grabbed his arm, spun him around and told him to try me. He did. He swung, I took a half step back, then laid my stick on his head right above his left ear. He went down in a heap, out cold. His mistake and mine: his because he took a swing at me; mine because I laid him out. His brother was a ward captain and I got ten days off without pay. Politics. By the time the ten days were up, I had a job collecting bad accounts for a bank and there were a lot of them in 1935. Lousy job, but for over a year, it paid the bills.

In 1937, I wangled a job working high steel on two buildings under construction in Chicago. Don't ask how. I lied a lot. It was great till cold weather set in. You don't know what cold is till you're twenty stories up on naked steel with the temperature at zero and the wind blowing thirty miles per hour. Hell, a stream of piss froze before it hit the beam. I headed back to New York and looked for a job in a nice warm department store. I didn't find one but someone told me I had a knack for figuring things out so why didn't I become a private investigator? I had enough money from the construction job to tide me over for a while and decided to give it a try. So there you are.

And here I was. I'd been waiting on a bus ten minutes and had just knocked the ash out of my pipe when one came along. It was less than a fifteen minute ride to Dumont where I could catch a trolley but time to relax and watch the city go by. Some of the stores had decorated for Christmas and there were folks on the street looking in store windows at things I suspected they couldn't afford to buy. Times were still tough. Roosevelt was trying but it wasn't enough. Unemployment was at its worst in 1937 and now, in 1939, ten years after the crash, it was still over seventeen percent. The only thing that would drag us out of the depression was a war that everyone knew was coming, but no one publically wanted to admit. I began to wonder if I'd try to enlist if it came. Probably too old. And if they did take me, all the young whippersnappers would call me Pop. Jesus! That's all I'd need!

I was still smiling at the thought when I got off the bus. There was an older, poorly dressed, woman with a frayed canvas satchel on her shoulder who I assumed was waiting on a trolley, so I asked how long it would be before one came that would take me along Dumont to Hinsdale. She said about fifteen minutes so I stepped into a nearby deli for a coffee. When I came out, I was just about to fill my pipe when a trolley came along and the woman pointed to it. I tipped my hat and got on board. She was still waiting. If she was still there on my way back, maybe I'd ask her what she was waiting for.

It was just a short ride. I walked north on Hinsdale a half block to Ariella's apartment building, stepped into the alcove and rang the buzzer for 2B. After a few seconds, her voice came over the intercom.

"Who is it?"

"Max Grant. I'm a few minutes early."

"That's alright. I'll come down."

When she opened the door I almost forgot why I was there. She was beyond attractive in a pale blue dress, tall at about five feet seven, straw-blonde, hazel eyes, early thirties, and a figure that would have shamed a bathing suit.

"Please come in, Mr. Grant."

"Thank you. I appreciate you seeing me on such short notice."

She nodded her head. I followed her upstairs and had the pleasure of watching poetry in motion. By the time we reached the front door of her apartment I knew I'd follow her anywhere. Down, Max-Down, boy!

She motioned to a chair across from a coffee table. "Please have a seat, Mr. Grant. I just made a pot of coffee. Would you like some?" Her accent, certainly German, was more noticeable than on the phone but her English was excellent. Seemed like I was running into a lot of Europeans lately. And like any red blooded American male, I noticed she wasn't wearing a wedding ring.

"That would be nice—just black." Even though I'd had a cup at the deli, I figured she'd gone to the trouble to make it, knowing I'd arrive about noon, and I was in a "polite" mood. My next thought was that I was in love for the second time in less than a week. Maybe I'd do well to check out the working girls in my neighborhood. Take the edge off.

She walked down a short hallway to the kitchen and I could hear cups and saucers rattling. She was back in a moment with coffee for both of us.

She sat on the sofa across from me and took a sip of coffee. "Now, Mr. Grant, you are looking for Sarah Bennett?"

"Yes. She arrived several days ago on the French Liner, De Grasse from Le Havre, but has not been seen since she left the arrivals area at the port. Has she been here?"

"No, though she was supposed to call me after she checked into the Savoy-Plaza. We were to have dinner. I phoned the hotel late in the evening and they told me they were holding a reservation for her but she hadn't checked in. I phoned again the day after and was told the same. At the time, I assumed she had remained in France for some reason."

"You knew she was in France?"

"I received a cable from her two weeks ago giving the date she was to arrive and said to plan to have dinner together that evening."

"Do you have the cable?"

"No, I noted the date on my calendar and threw it away."

"Do you know what she did? For a living, I mean."

"She dealt in art, primarily European artists, some known, some unknown. She sometimes took requests from American collectors, but most often, just bought there and sent or brought the works back here to be placed in galleries for sale. She visited several European countries a couple times a year: France, Belgium, Sweden, Holland, Denmark. In the past, she occasionally traveled to Germany. I don't think she has this year, but I could be wrong. Hitler, you know . . . ." She grimaced and paused for a few seconds. "She usually managed to visit England as well. She loved England. I think she'd like to live there."

"Does she speak languages other than English?"

"French, German, and Dutch. All quite well. She minored in languages in college."

"You knew her then?"

"We were in City College together and have remained close friends since. She went on to get a graduate degree in mathematics. I stopped when they handed me my bachelor's diploma."

"Now I'm going to ask you a leading question. Do you know if she ever dealt in anything other than art?"

"Like what?"

"Like carrying messages from Europe to America or vise-versa."

"You mean to and from refugee families?"

"Perhaps to and from members of scientific or educational communities."

"I know she visited friends at Princeton and on several occasions, Columbia University. She taught mathematics at Princeton for a short time. Mr. Grant, before we talk further, how is it you are concerned with looking for Sarah?"

"I was asked."

"And who asked you? Was it someone from one of the universities?"

"No . . . It was a dead man." Her eyes widened and she sat back on the sofa.

"What do you mean?"

"Do you know a Dane named Hans Moller?"

"No."

"I found Hans Moller several nights ago in an alley in lower Manhattan. He was dying from two gunshot wounds to the chest. He asked me to find Sarah Bennett and then died." I didn't want to get into any detail about the cigarette case. "I learned the following day he had visited Princeton and that's how I discovered Sarah's connection with the University. They expected to see her soon after her arrival but she didn't show up. And as I said on the phone, they asked me to look into her disappearance."

She didn't say anything for a minute, just stared at the hallway to the kitchen. Finally, she said, "It must be something happened to her. You checked hospitals?"

"Princeton did."

"Is there anything I can do to help?"

"You already have. You've given me a more rounded picture of her than I had."

"If you think I can help in any way, or if you find her, please phone me."

"I will, I promise. Oh, I meant to ask you . . . In the phone book you're listed as GA Blumfeld. What does the G stand for?"

"Gisela. I am German. I came here from Coburg, in Bavaria, with my younger brother Johan and our grandparents as a child of twelve. My parents were killed in a train accident when I was very small. We were raised by my father's parents."

"Your brother live in New York as well?"

"In Yonkers. But—" She hesitated. "But he changed his name to Vogel, John Vogel, a couple years ago. He said Blumfeld sounded too Jewish." She smiled. "I guess it does. We were raised Jewish but neither of us have been practicing Jews for years. I simply don't go to temple, but my brother distains everything Jewish. He works for a large hat manufacturer and gets into the city occasionally." She paused again. "Truthfully, he may get into the city often but I wouldn't know. He did stop by last month but that's the first time I'd seen him since early in the year."

"You don't get along?"

"We don't see eye to eye on some things. Politics in particular."

"Democrat and Republican?"

"European politics. He is very German."

"I see." I set my cup on the table and stood. "Well, thank you for everything, Miss Blumfeld."

She held out her hand. "Ari, my friends call me Ari."

I smiled as I shook her hand. "And mine call me Max."

I snagged a trolley just as I hit the corner of Hinsdale and Dumont and dropped off at 98th. It was now after one o'clock and my morning Danish didn't stretch that far so I stopped in the deli where I'd had coffee earlier. I ordered pastrami and swiss on rye with a Coke. While waiting on my order I looked around. Lo and behold, the old lady I'd seen at the trolley stop out front was nursing a cup of coffee at a table. I debated asking her what she was waiting for but vetoed the thought. Hell, maybe she was counting trolleys . . . or busses. More likely, she was collecting betting or numbers slips. I shrugged. None of my business.

TWELVE

Back in my office before two-thirty, I shed my coat, scarf and hat, and then stood in front of my open stash cabinet as if I were a Buddhist having a vision. I must have stared into the cabinet for a full minute, mind blank, before taking a glass and pouring a couple ounces of rye into it. I picked a Lucky out of the pack, went to my desk, sat, and lit the cigarette. It tasted rank in comparison to my pipe. After a couple puffs, I put it out, went to my coat, took out my pipe, filled and lit it. Taste and aroma were sweet. I took a sip of rye and called my answering service. No messages.

Ari. Ari Blumfeld. Nice name for a nice woman. I suspected she was Jewish and she had confirmed it. Not that it mattered to me. I was ecumenical as hell when it came to women, though I drew the line at witches and devil worshipers. Pointy hats and bizarre mumbo jumbo complicated the romantic side of a relationship, not to mention the vision of a black cat, claws bared, leaping onto the middle of my bare back while making love. I chuckled at the thought. Sure would make orgasm a flash in the pan.

I was antsy. Setting my pipe in the ashtray, I picked up my glass and wandered around my office and then to the front room that was Pepper's domain. There was an article on her desk, apparently cut from a newspaper a few months before. I read the headline upside down: "London Prepares For War." It sounded interesting so I sat at her desk and read it.

London Prepares For War
By: Mollie Panter-Downes for the New Yorker Magazine
September 8, 1939

On the stretch of green turf by Knightsbridge Barracks, which used to be the scampering ground for the smartest terriers in London, has appeared a row of steam shovels that bite out mouthfuls of earth, hoist it aloft, and dump it into lorries; it is then carted away to fill sandbags. The eye has now become accustomed to sandbags everywhere, and to the balloon barrage, the trap for enemy planes, which one morning spread over the sky like some form of silvery dermatitis.

Gas masks have suddenly become part of everyday civilian equipment and everybody is carrying the square cardboard cartons that look as though they might contain a pound of grapes for a sick friend. Bowlegged admirals stump jauntily up Whitehall with their gas masks slung neatly in knapsacks over their shoulders. Last night London was completely blacked out. A few cars crawled through the streets with one headlight out and the other hooded while Londoners, suddenly become homebodies . . .

The evacuation of London, which is to be spaced over three days, began yesterday and was apparently a triumph for all concerned. At seven o'clock in the morning all inward traffic was stopped and A.A. scouts raced through the suburbs whisking shrouds of sacking off imposing bulletin boards, which informed motorists that all the principal routes out of town were one-way streets for three days. Cars poured out pretty steadily all day yesterday and today, packed with people, luggage, children's perambulators, and domestic pets, but the congestion at busy points was no worse than it is at any other time in the holiday season. The railways, whose workers had been on the verge of going out on strike when the crisis came, played their part nobly and the London stations, accustomed to receiving trainloads of child refugees from the Third Reich, got down to the job of dispatching trainload after trainload of children the other way-this time, cheerful little cockneys who ordinarily get to the country perhaps once a year on the local church outing and could hardly believe the luck that was sending them now. Left behind, the mothers stood around rather listlessly at street corners waiting for the telegrams that were to be posted up at the various schools to tell them where their children were.

Although the summer holiday is still on, village schools have reopened as centers where the evacuated hordes from London can be rested, sorted out, medically examined, refreshed with tea and biscuits, and distributed to their new homes. The war has brought the great unwashed right into the bosoms of the great washed; while determined ladies in white V.A.D. overalls search the mothers' heads with a knitting needle for unwelcome signs of life, the babies are dandled and patted on their often grimy diapers by other ladies, who have been told to act as hostesses and keep the guests from pining for Shoreditch.

Guest rooms have been cleared of Crown Derby knickknacks and the best guest towels, and the big houses and cottages alike are trying to overcome the traditional British dislike of strangers, who may, for all anybody knows, be parked in them for a matter of years, not weeks.

Today was a day of unprecedented activity in the air. Squadrons of bombers bustled in all directions and at midday an enormous number of vast planes, to which the knowing pointed as troop-carriers, droned overhead toward an unknown destination that was said by two sections of opinion to be (a) France and (b) Poland. On the ground, motor buses full of troops in bursting good humor tore through the villages, the men waving at the girls and howling "Tipperary" and other ominously dated ditties that everybody has suddenly remembered and found to be as good for a war in 1939 as they were in 1914

London and the country are buzzing with rumors, a favorite one being that Hitler carries a gun in his pocket and means to shoot himself if things don't go too well; another school of thought favors the version that he is now insane and Goring has taken over . . . The English were a peace-loving nation up to two days ago, but now it is pretty widely felt that the sooner we really get down to the job, the better.

Pretty mild, I thought, but much has happened in the three months since this article appeared in the Times. Poland surrendered and was divided by Germany and the Soviet Union, the British sent 150,000 troops to France, and someone tried to knock off Hitler with a bomb in a Munich beer hall. It's a shame they missed. The Soviet Union attacked Finland at the end of November but last I heard on the radio, they were having a hard time. The Finns must be tougher than anyone thought. I had no doubt we'd get into this mess sooner or later but a lot will depend on how well or badly Britain fares in the coming months. Rumors circulate that Roosevelt is trying to quietly work around the official American position of neutrality and that's probably true.

The phone rang.

"Grant Agency."

"It's Murphy, Max. I have some information but not a helluva lot. I must have talked to a dozen porters at the port of entry till I found one who happened to be standing out front and saw Sarah Bennett get into a taxi with a man. He said he wouldn't have paid much attention but when he offered his services to the man while inside the building, the fellow was nasty and curt with him. The porter connected with someone else and that's the reason he was out front and saw them get a taxi. Last taxi for a few minutes in fact, till several more queued up. Also, he said there was something odd about the taxi. It was a Checker, alright, but didn't seem to have a company name or number on it. But he also said it was raining pretty hard and he just might have missed it. I asked if he thought the man and woman knew each other and he said no, he heard the man say something about it being the last taxi and offered to share a ride with the woman.

"I also walked a couple blocks in each direction thinking I might see something, maybe the taxi, but didn't see much of interest except for some empty warehouses and some other rundown buildings. Ya know, Max, I got a feeling like it might be worthwhile to spend more time in the dock area. I can arrange to take Tuesday off if you'd like me to wander around here a bit more. Might be able to find some street people or hobos who've seen the taxi and the couple in it. There's some railway spur lines that butt up against the dock area just a block away."

"That'd be great, Murph, if you could manage it, but I don't want you to do anything that might screw up your retirement."

"Shouldn't be a problem. Doubt they'll miss me. I have a couple weeks of vacation coming they're going to have to pay me for anyway."

"Good enough. Keep track of your hours and if you have something to eat while you're looking, that goes on the bill, too. I'll pay you next Friday."

"Okay. I'll head for home now. See ya Tuesday."

I hung up the phone, killed the rest of the rye, and then noticed a two day old copy of the Herald Tribune in Pepper's waste basket. I pulled it out and flipped through the pages. A list of movies caught my eye and one in particular drew my attention: *Confessions Of A Nazi Spy* with Edward G. Robinson and George Sanders. The thought crossed my mind to phone Ari to ask if she'd like to see it, but I decided against it. Two reasons: I didn't know her well enough, and it just didn't seem like the kind of film she'd enjoy. I was probably wrong on both counts, but decisions are often made that way.

I decided I'd like to see it, checked the show times, and found there was an early evening showing I could follow up with dinner somewhere. Afterwards, I'd come home to a bourbon, a pipe, a book, some radio, and to sleep. And that's what I did.

THIRTEEN

For Sarah Bennett, the days crept unpleasantly by. For a while, she wasn't sure how many. With no window, watch or clock, days and nights had no meaning in her cell. She could have called it her room, but cell was more appropriate. But now she knew it had been five days since she arrived in New York. Today was Sunday. Sunday, unless distant church bells rang for some other reason. She'd heard two distinct tones about an hour apart. And now that she knew the day, she could account for what had taken place since she'd been kidnaped. Well, almost.

That first day she had only had bread and tea during the day but in the evening, Smith Number One brought her more tea with a swiss cheese sandwich and dill pickle that had obviously come from a deli. She wondered if the deli were nearby and considered that if it were, it might tell her where she was located. Then again, probably not unless she could learn the name. New York had hundreds of delis. Smith said nothing till he stopped at the door and turned.

"You will be here a while. My cont . . ." He paused, then started again. "I am told the gentleman you asked about earlier is currently unavailable for a week to ten days." He said nothing more and left her wondering what he'd started to say. Contact? Controller?

The atmosphere of the room matched the demeanor of the Smiths—gray and grim. On the next day, she asked Smith Number One for something to read. He didn't reply but some time later, Number Two entered, set a Gideon Bible and an old Sunday New York Times Magazine on the table and left without saying a word. She wondered what hotel they'd stolen the bible from. She was not a religious person but at least it was something to read. She would save the NYT magazine for later and just read several pages per day.

Some things had become routine. Each morning after breakfast, which now consisted of a boiled egg along with bread and tea, Smith Number Two would silently enter, pick up the toilet bucket and leave, returning with the rinsed and empty bucket ten minutes later. They had also found a slightly larger board to cover it with when not in use. Lunch and dinner always consisted of a sandwich, most often cheese, but twice, it had been pastrami, and almost always her meals were brought by Smith Number One.

On the following morning as he was turning to leave, she said, "I would like to have a bath." He paused and looked at her. Not a look of astonishment but more one of surprise as if the thought of a bath had never occurred to him. After a few seconds he told her that a bath was impossible and then left without another word. Thinking about it later, she realized he might have been embarrassed.

But forty minutes later, both Smiths were back, Smith Number One carrying a towel and bar of soap and Smith Number Two with two buckets of hot water. Number One set the towel and soap on the table and Number Two set the buckets of water next to it. Number One said, "You may wash." And they left. She removed her blouse and bra and washed her upper body using one-third of the towel wet and the other two-thirds to dry with. Glancing over her shoulder to make sure the slot in the door was closed, she dropped her skirt and underpants to wash "the nasty bits" as the British were fond of saying. If anyone would have told her washing with two buckets of hot water could be luxurious, she would have said they were nuts. But it was.

By Sunday, midday, she'd made up her mind to confront Smith Number One in some small way but also realized doing so might make things more difficult for her. They could cut off her food and drink, not empty her waste bucket, any number of things, but somehow she felt that wouldn't happen. When Number One brought her sandwich, she spoke.

"Where is your boss that he can't visit his prisoner?"

He didn't reply immediately but after a few seconds shrugged his shoulders and said, "He is not in the country at the moment but should return in five or six days."

"Where is he?"

Another pause, another shrug, and a slight smile as if it didn't matter. And she knew why it didn't matter. Either way, information or no information, she'd never leave this place alive.

"He is in South America . . . Brazil and Argentina."

"Why?"

"That, I'm afraid, Miss Bennett, I cannot answer." He left abruptly without saying another word or giving her an opportunity to ask another question.

Can't answer or won't answer, she thought. Her guess was he didn't know but she suspected she did. The man in charge was higher up on the food chain than she originally thought. South America, mainly Brazil and Argentina, had about one and a half million German emigrants, most living in enclaves and most supporting the Fatherland openly or clandestinely. South America was fast becoming a staging ground for Nazi spies to infiltrate America. Rio de Janeiro and Buenos Aires would become hubs for sending and receiving information from Germany, if they haven't already. The world was crawling with spies and the Nazis would consider her one, if not formally, then certainly by her actions.

She glanced at the Gideon Bible. The use of spies had a long history going back to Moses or even before. Soon after the Israelites left Egypt, Moses sent twelve spies into Canaan to report on its weaknesses and strengths. They were gone forty days and when they returned it was with bad news: Canaan would be a tough nut to crack. The Israelites wanted a new leader and rebelled but Moses managed to remain in power. He then told them as punishment for their rebellion, they would wander in the desert one year for every day the spies were gone. Forty. The old goat was a hard taskmaster, almost as crotchety as his god who destroyed cities and populations because he was in a snit.

Ah well . . . Spies and espionage weren't really her affair though she had to admit she had apparently fallen into a nest of them. She didn't see herself as a spy, though certain others, particularly the Nazis, would take a different view. She didn't have a formal mission or specific task, and didn't have contact with anyone in any government. She simply facilitated the sharing of information among the international scientific community. Because of the war in Europe and the political atmosphere in some countries, scientists often had a difficult time meeting outside their own countries. As an art dealer, she could travel rather freely, though of late, it was becoming more difficult.

The thought of art led her back to Hans Moller. Eventually, she'd have to explain that connection to whoever was in charge of Smith and Smith. Why meet in the States when Moller was a Dane and she had been in Denmark? She could say that at the time she briefly met him in Copenhagen, she mentioned the Picasso and her intention to buy, but the picture was in France and she wasn't going to make an offer till she was on her way back to America. He offered to meet her in New York because he was going to be there for several weeks, during which time, she would be returning on the De Grasse. If she was assertive enough, the story was just plausible. They might believe it.

She didn't like Moller and suspected he worked both sides of the fence. A mercenary in the spy business who was for sale to the highest bidder. Hell, he was probably wondering where she was, maybe even looking for her. Wandering around the dock area. She doubted he'd go to the police. That might open too many doors he wished would remain closed. She chuckled. Bet he's pissed, she thought. She knew he wouldn't be paid till he could negotiate a price through her for whatever information it was he was carrying. She would take it to the group at Princeton along with the sheets she had hidden in her boots. They would determine its value. She was never paid for information. They simply financed her art purchases. She repaid the purchase price and pocked the profit from sales.

Hmmm . . . She returned to the thought of wandering around the dock area. The next time Smith Number One brought her food, she'd ask about some exercise. She could fake getting a cough, not feeling well and complain it's the result of the stale air in her cell. Tell him she needed some fresh air and exercise. Might or might not work but it was worth a try.

FOURTEEN

Yawn . . . Sunday mornings are for lying in bed and letting the mind wander. Mine was wandering all over hell's half acre. I was thinking about changing Grant Agency to Grant Investigations. Made sense. Grant Agency could be an insurance company or modeling agency. I'd ask Pepper what she thought. She has a good, common sense feel for things like that.

Confessions of a Nazi Spy was a good film, or at least I thought so. Part documentary style and part story, and I'm not sure either part was fiction. Edward G. Robinson, who plays an FBI agent doesn't enter the film till about half way through it but was totally believable. George Sanders plays a Nazi stooge, a disappointment for me because I really like him and wanted him to be one of the good guys. Excellent performance as always, though. Afterward, I had a good spaghetti dinner at a small out of the way place about a block from the theater. I didn't remember the name of the half bottle of wine I had with the dinner but it was smooth and tart at the same time. When I go back, I'll ask.

But it was the walk of a few blocks back to my office that proved interesting. It was snowing, not hard, though steady, and I thought about taking a taxi but the temperature was just below freezing with no wind and the wine with dinner provided a warm insulator. I was walking across an alleyway when I heard a bang. Not a gunshot but the sound of something slamming into metal. I stopped and looked. Just looked. My last encounter in an alley was still fresh in my memory and would probably remain there forever. I wasn't seeking chapter two of that story. But I heard the bang again and this time there was a moan behind it.

What the hell, in for a penny, in for a pound, as my limey friend Harry Wilson says. I slipped my .38 from my shoulder rig into my coat pocket and kept my hand on it. A bit less than 100 feet into the alley there was a large trash receptacle with two smaller cans beside it. Something banging against the cans or the receptacle was the only thing I could think of that would make the sound I heard. I stayed against the far building wall and walked slowly toward the cans, the couple inches of snow muffling my steps.

There wasn't much light, just a fan type streetlight about fifty feet beyond the cans but the snow reflected it well. "Good shooting light," I murmured, and then, "Where the hell did that thought come from?" I shrugged. When I got to a point just a few feet beyond the cans, I could see two guys working a fellow over who was on the ground. One of the two was leaning against the building, and the other had the guy on the ground by the coat front, setting up to slam him into the receptacle again.

I stepped away from the wall at my back. "Need some help?"

The leaning one came off the building fast. "Wha chu mean, fucker? We don need help."

"I wasn't talking to you. I was talking to the man on the ground."

"Fuck off, man, or get cut." He started toward me, large switchblade in hand. I backed to the building wall till I came up against it. The second guy who'd been beating the fellow on the ground was now standing and grinning.

I let the guy get to within six feet when I pulled my .38, stepped forward, swung it in an arc and smashed it against the left side of his head. He went down hard. I slammed my foot down on his wrist and the knife slid a couple feet away. His junior partner pulled a butterfly knife, flicked it open and started for me so I stooped, jammed my revolver against my guy's neck and said, "Tell your buddy to stop or I'll blow your goddam head off!"

"Jesus, Marko, stop! Stop!"

I was grinning. "OK, Marko, drop the knife like a good boy and I'll let your buddy get up."

The knife dropped and I stepped back. The fellow I'd clocked got to his hands and knees and then slowly stood.

I put on my rugged, tough guy act and in a gruff whiskey voice said, "You have two choices: die here, or walk down the alley to the far end staying in the middle so I can get a good clean shot if I change my mind." They walked. Well, one walked and the other staggered a bit.

I waited till they got to the end of the alley and disappeared around the corner of the last building before I checked on the fellow they were playing happy time with. He was sitting up against the trash receptacle and I could see in the snow reflected light he was negro, maybe fifty years old or older. His nose was bleeding slightly, and he had a nasty scrape on his right cheek where they must have slammed his head into the side of the receptacle. I reached out my hand.

"Can you walk?"

"Dunno. Think so." he grabbed my hand, got to his feet, then took a couple steps back and leaned against the building.

"Thanks, mister . . . ?"

"Grant, Max Grant."

"Thanks, Mister Grant. They was looking to work me over then cut me. Ida bled to death here in this alley."

"What'd you do to piss 'em off?"

"Owed 'em money. Not them, the guy they work for."

"How much?"

"Twenty bucks."

"Damn! Nasty payback for twenty bucks."

"Yeah, well . . . they was settin' to make an example of the nigger. Word gets around. Others pay up fast."

I put the .38 back in my shoulder rig. "Can you make it out to the street? Make it home?"

"Yeah. Ribs hurt, too, but I don't think broke. I'll be alright."

We walked slowly back the way I came. "None of my business but why'd you owe twenty bucks.? That's not a helluva lot of money."

"To you, maybe, but I been outta work a couple months. Got a seven year old granddaughter livin' with me. Her mother, my daughter, died a couple year ago and I been raisin' the girl best I can. We get food at the mission or one of the kitchens, but she needs some warm clothes. An' I thought with Christmas comin' on I'd get her some little thing. Borrowed fifteen bucks. Payback is twenty after seven days. Thought I could get some day work. Didn't."

"Did you get the clothes?"

"Yeah, an' a nice doll for a dollar."

We got to the street and stopped. "What's your name?"

"Herb. Herb Spenser."

"They going to be looking for you again, Herb?"

"Maybe in a day or two."

I pulled out my wallet, fished out twenty-five bucks and my card and handed it to him.

"I can't be takin' your money, mister. You done enough."

"Take it. Pay the twenty to the shark and get a decent dinner for you and your granddaughter for Christmas."

"I can't pay you back."

"I didn't ask. But it comes with a couple strings attached. I've been where you are or damned near, so first off, if you find yourself in the chips someday and run across some down-and-out, pass on the twenty-five. Second, come up to my office one day next week and maybe we can find some work for you."

He glanced at my card. "We?"

"Yeah. My associate's name is Pepper. She's smarter than I am. Might know of some work."

He reached out his hand. "I don't know how to thank you."

"Don't. Merry Christmas."

Twenty minutes later I was back in my own digs and happy to be there.

Now morning, I thought about that encounter a bit. It could have gone bad in a lot of ways, too many to even think about. One thing I was pleased with, was not having to fire my revolver. Not only would it have involved a lot of explanation but also a lot of paperwork and a lengthy stint with the DA. It did prove one thing, though: Sometimes the threat of deadly force is as good, or better, than the use of force itself.

Next on my list of mind wanderings was Sarah Bennett. I wondered if she was still alive and if so, where. My thoughts then turned to Smith and Smith, and I played "what if" with that for a few minutes. They were hunting information carried by Moller. What if they already had part of the information because they had taken it from Bennett and needed Moller's part? What if Pepper's idea of putting an ad in the newspaper wasn't such a bad idea? Hell, I even gave it some credence at the time but put it off for a couple days. Then two really important ideas came to me: A pot of coffee, and a shower. All else immediately went to the back burner.

I made a pot of coffee and took a steaming cup with me to the shower stall. No, not inside, but to the back of the toilet. I took a sip after I toweled off. Just the right drinking temperature. I shaved, trimmed my mustache which was beginning to look like the un-mowed grass that pops up through cracks in the sidewalk, and got dressed. Sunday or not, I put on my shoulder rig with my .38 in it. I didn't want to be caught empty handed again, so to speak. Before going into my office, I turned the radio on just loud enough that I could hear it from the next room.

It was almost nine o'clock. Just in time for news and weather.

At my desk, I picked up my pipe, cleaned the dottle out of the bowl and filled it with Edgeworth. It suddenly dawned on me that my smoking routine in the morning had changed. Until a short time ago, my first action on waking was to put my feet on the floor and reach for my pack of Luckys on the bedside table. I hadn't really noticed the change till just now. I lit the pipe, took a few puffs, and listened to the radio.

The weather was the same as it had been for a couple days: rain mixed with snow, changing to all snow later in the day. I had no plans other than one trip outside for brunch, and a sandwich to go for dinner. It was a good day to stay warm inside and maybe take a nap.

National news was a bit dull with the exception of one item: Roosevelt unveiled a new policy that would embargo supplies to nations targeting civilians and who violate other accepted rules of engagement. Someone had termed it a moral embargo. Call it what you will, it was aimed at Germany and Japan. They knew it and we knew it.

Our Canadian neighbors sent more than seven thousand troops to Britain to assist their war effort. It didn't seem like much to me but considering Canada's population, it might be a lot. And they were talking about the sinking of the German battleship, Graf Spee, off the coast of Montevideo. It wasn't actually sunk by the British, it was scuttled by its Captain, Langsdorff, after being damaged in an engagement with three British warships on the thirteenth. The war in Europe was going badly for the allies on all fronts, and I thought about that. The western nations involved in the fight against the Nazis, sans America, were playing catch-up and not doing it very well. They had dithered and neglected their own military capabilities while Hitler rebuilt his war machine. Thank God there were signs Roosevelt was taking the threat seriously. I was certain we'd be in it up to our necks eventually but how or when, no one knew.

Locally, things seemed to be reasonably quiet. The subway project was running ahead of schedule in spite of the weather. I smiled at that. Stands to reason—most of the work is underground. The new La Guardia Airport that opened on the 2nd with an inaugural flight from Chicago was doing a roaring business. And there was a short commentary on the borough photography project that was progressing well. That one, I'd never heard of but the project involved photographing all the homes and buildings in the five boroughs. It was estimated to take two to three years. No reason given, but I suspect it had to do with taxes. The city is always looking for ways to squeeze an extra drop of blood from its inhabitants.

I walked back to the bedroom and turned the dial on the radio searching for some music. I caught a few seconds of Gene Autry singing *Back In The Saddle Again* and kept turning. It'd been so long since I'd been in the saddle, I didn't need reminding. I finally found Glenn Miller playing *Sunrise Serenade* and left it there. My mind conjured up a connection between Back In The Saddle and Sunrise Serenade but I liked the song and figured it would be followed by more of the same. I was right. Back in my office warming up my coffee I heard the beginning of *Address Unknown* by The Ink Spots.

The mind is a strange thing. It has a mind of its own. And no, I wasn't going to follow that crazy thought anywhere. But prompted by *Address Unknown*, my thoughts turned back to Sarah Bennett. Why I had the feeling she was still alive, I don't know. Logically, if she was kidnapped for information, they'd had plenty of time to wring it out of her, and if they had, they weren't going to turn her loose to walk to the closest precinct station. Call it what you will, but I just had that gut feeling she was alive and in the city somewhere, feeling helpless and hopeless. Helpless and hopeless is just about the way I felt. I had damned little to go on. Hell, I had nothing to go on. Oh, I had background information, connections, friends, but nothing to point me in the direction I needed to look for her. I needed a break, even a manufactured one.

Smith and Smith! Had to be. I'd run an ad in bold print in the personals in several newspapers. Just a simple ad: "Smith and Smith Contact Grant" with my office phone number. That should do it if they read newspapers and I suspected they did. Pepper could do that first thing in the morning to catch the afternoon editions and following morning ones as well. It was worth a try. And if they show up, then what? Well, I'd work that out later.

FIFTEEN

Emit Fielding felt like shit. He had stopped by the dispensary Saturday after meeting with Professor von Neumann, was examined by a doctor and given some pills: aspirin and some new sulfa drug. Neither seemed to have much effect though he imagined the aspirin kept his fever at bay. The doctor said he should see some improvement in forty-eight hours but it was now Monday and he didn't feel much better. "Count your blessings, old man," he muttered, "at least you don't feel worse."

The doctor also said he didn't think it was pneumonia but simply a bad chest cold. The sulfa drug was just a precaution according to him. Truth be told, he got more comfort and relief from the stiff hot toddy he fixed for himself Saturday evening and again Sunday evening. At least he was able to sleep several hours each night without waking to a racking cough.

He was still in his pajamas and robe. A widower, he lived alone and "did for himself" as some of his British colleagues were wont to say. This morning, after black coffee, a slice of toast, and pills, he phoned the institute to let them know he wouldn't be in. The telephone party line he shared with two other residences was clear for a change. The two were unknown to him but one of them had children who seemed to tie up the phone for hours on end.

After listening to his raspy voice and cough, the secretary he spoke with sounded eminently grateful. No more than myself, he thought. Before returning to bed, he went to his den, selected a couple books from the bookcase and two files from his desk. The first book was a translation of essays by Niels Bohr on atomic physics and the second was a mathematics and physics dictionary and glossary. The files simply contained papers by scientists like von Neumann, Einstein, Lise Meitner, Fermi, and others he had collected over the past couple of years.

Bohr, like Einstein, had a remarkable genius for insight. He had made foundational contributions to understanding atomic structure and quantum mechanics, and received the Nobel Prize in Physics in 1922 for his work. He collaborated with many of the top physicists in Europe and the United States and often invited them to his institute in Copenhagen. To both Bohr and Einstein, some things, while unproven, were intuitively obvious. Using their imagination, they would propose a hypothesis and then set out to prove it. They generally succeeded. Bohr, however, being in Copenhagen, would sooner or later be a target of the Nazis. Fielding suspected they would try to use him, and failing that, would kill him. He wondered if Bohr had ever considered leaving his homeland. If so, he hoped he would come to the United States.

Fielding would reread the most recent papers of Einstein and Bohr but the material that interested him most was that of Lise Meitner who could rightly be called one of the most brilliant physicists of the young twentieth century. Though in her sixties, she and Otto

Frisch had developed the first theory of nuclear fission in 1938. More remarkable to Fielding than her discoveries, was the fact that she was able to attain a doctor's degree in physics at a time when women were not permitted to attend any institute of higher learning in Vienna or much of Europe.

Fielding paged through one of the files till he came to a hand written summary of Meitner. Though it was not signed, he suspected it had been written by Professor von Neumann.

After she was awarded her doctorate degree in 1906, she went to the Kaiser Wilhelm Institute for Chemistry in Berlin where she studied and worked with Max Planck and the chemist Otto Hahn. There she remained for thirty years and led a section at the Institute. When Austria was annexed by Germany in 1938, Meitner was forced to flee Germany for Sweden. Though Austrian and a Christian convert, she was born Jewish which undoubtedly made her a target for the Nazis. They confiscated her passport but she still managed to escape. She continued her work at Siegbahn's institute in Stockholm, but with little support, partially due to Siegbahn's prejudice against women in science. She and Hahn met secretly in November, 1938 in Copenhagen and planned experiments that provided evidence for nuclear fission. The results of those experiments were published in January, 1939. In February, Meitner, with her nephew, Otto Frisch, described the process in a letter to the journal Nature and named the process nuclear fission. She also predicted the existence of a nuclear chain reaction. It was this published work that led Albert Einstein to write his letter to President Roosevelt.

It was a good summary. Condensed, but good. He flipped through a few more pages, thinking he might find the article from Nature, or at least an extract, but there was none. But the summary bore out what Von Neumann had said when they met on Saturday: the Germans had the scientists and the information that could lead to a nuclear bomb. The question was, how far along they were in the process and what effort would they put into development. Sarah Bennett, if she were still alive and could be found, might have the answers.

SIXTEEN

I know there are people who complain about Monday mornings, but I'm not one of them, at least not anymore. Back when I was working for someone else, I did my share of complaining, but that was before I became an investigator. Since then, each Monday morning has become a new adventure or a continuing adventure from the previous week.

I was sitting at my desk waiting on our coffee and Danish delivery from the deli and lighting my morning pipe when Pepper came through the door. "Don't take your hat off, good-looking, I've got a chore for you this morning."

"I ain't wearin' a hat, boss."

"That's okay, you don't have to go back out either."

"Man, are you screwed up. Have bedroom company last night?"

"No, but I had a vision."

"Jesus! Da Man been smoking weed."

"Nope. Bourbon."

"You were smoking bourbon?"

"Something tells me this conversation, which started out on a downhill slide, is now gaining momentum."

"Wanna start again?"

"Yeah. You know that idea you had about putting an ad in the newspaper for Smith and Smith? Well, I think it's a good one. Put it in the Times, the Herald, and a couple more you can think of. Bold and caps. All it has to read is,

SMITH AND SMITH PHONE GRANT, just as I've written here. Add our office number." I got up from my desk and handed her a piece of paper from my note pad.

"Think that'll do it, huh?"

"If they see it, it will. Bet on it."

"Whatcha wanna bet?"

"Lunch."

"You're on."

She took off her coat and scarf, hung them on the rack, sat down and pulled the phone book from her desk drawer.

I turned to go back in my office but paused. "Did the DA say what he wanted when he called Friday?"

"Nope. Just said for you to call."

"Okay, I'll do that now."

Assistant DA Smith picked up on the second ring. His voice sounded gravely like he'd had a rough weekend or hadn't had his daily ruben sandwich yet.

"DA's office, Smith."

"Max Grant. You called Friday?"

"Sure took your time getting back to me. Out getting laid somewhere?"

"Yeah. Eight times. Jealous?"

"You're a goddam wiseass, Grant, you know that?"

"I've heard it before. Why the call, Smith?"

"Just thought you'd like some additional information on that guy Moller who caught the double tap last week. Seems like you and Sergeant Belden both missed a witness."

"A witness? Who?"

"Some wino living in a bunch of cardboard boxes at the far end of the alley. He saw Moller come into the alley and was going to hit him up for some change when he got to the wino's end, but about half way, someone stepped out of the shadows and demanded Moller's wallet. Or in the words of the wino, "Gimme your fucking wallet or you're dead." Moller took a swing at the guy and got shot for his trouble. The wino said he figured the shooter would search for Moller's wallet but instead, ducked back in a doorway and disappeared. Maybe went inside one of the buildings. Maybe shook up. Maybe scared. Maybe didn't mean to shoot Moller, but his hand was cold and it just happened.

"Lot of maybes."

"Yeah, but shit happens. The wino just covered up with a couple more boxes, and was there when you and Belden were, but didn't come out."

"So how'd you find this out?"

"Friday morning, Patrolman Howard was walking his regular beat that took him through the alley when out pops the wino from his temporary home. Scared the hell out of Howard. The wino said he had information on the shooting he'd sell for five bucks. Long story short: Howard called for Belden and Belden got it for two."

"Snitches are getting cheaper."

"Yeah . . . three bottles of wine."

I picked up my pipe and tamped the cold ash down with my finger. "So it was just a street heist gone bad. Is that what you think?"

"That's what it looks like. You think different?"

"No, not really. A witness is a witness. Wino or not, it sounds reliable." I struck a match and put it to my pipe. "I'm curious, though. Why tell me about it?"

"I wasn't going to, Grant. I don't like you. Belden is the one who suggested it. Said because you found Moller, you might want to know, and also that you're sometimes the source of good information. Ex-cop to cop, so to speak."

"Well, whether you like me or not, thank you. And tell Belden thank you. I appreciate it."

As I hung up, I mumbled, "Damn!" I said it again a few minutes later just as Pepper walked into my office.

What's the matter, boss, Smith give you a hard time?"

"No. I meant to ask if Howard was his first name or last or both."

"You mean Smith?"

"No, a beat cop in lower Manhattan."

"You lost me."

"The first cop on the scene of Moller's murder is named Howard. I was just curious as to whether it's his first name or last."

"Important?"

"Nope."

"Good. The Times and the Post will get your personal in this afternoon's edition. The Herald will carry it tomorrow. I didn't contact the Wall Street Journal. From your description of the Smith twins, I thought it would be a waste of money."

"I agree. But since we're talking money, let's get a contract off to Professor Fielding at Princeton."

"How should I make it out? I wouldn't think Fielding is our employer."

"Make it out to Princeton. If they want to change that, they can do it. Speaking of employers, if a down and out named Herb Spencer wanders in while I'm not here, I told him you might have a line on some work. Day-work, whatever. Anything he can do to pick up a few bucks."

"What the hell am I, the city employment agency?"

"No, but you always seem to know about such things. I never do."

"Just who is Herb Spencer?"

"Fellow I ran into in an alley Saturday night."

She stared at me for a full twenty seconds. "Do I want to know what you were doing in an alley Saturday night?"

"You might. I'll tell you over lunch."

"Spencer—He get shot, too?"

"Beat up. Does it make any difference?"

"Nope. Just curious."

"Curious is sometimes risky. Ask me."

There was a tap at the door and the kid from the deli came in, set a sack and two coffees on Pepper's desk, waved, and walked out. Pepper took a wrapped Danish from the sack, put it on her desk and brought the sack and the other coffee to me. Good thing. I was starved.

I had just finished my Danish when the phone rang. Pepper caught it, listened a few seconds, then said, "Just a moment, please." She stuck her head in my office, a smile on her face. "It's Ariella Blumfeld for you. Sounds nice. Are you sure you didn't have company last night?"

I grinned as I picked up the phone. Keep her guessing.

"Max Grant."

"Hello Max, its Ari. I've been thinking . . . thinking maybe I should go to the police precinct and report Sarah missing."

"I don't think that's a good idea, Ari, for two reasons. First, you don't have standing because you're not a relative. I'm sure they'd take a report but I doubt they'd put any effort into looking for her. She's an adult, and adults go missing all the time. And though we may suspect she's been taken by someone, we have no hard proof of that. Second is since I talked with you, there have been a couple developments. Look . . . what are you doing for lunch? I can pick you up and we can talk while we eat."

Silence. Then, "Why don't you come here for lunch. I just feel as though I should be doing something to find her."

"I understand. I really do. Lunch at your place is fine. What time?"

"One o'clock?"

"One will work. I'll see you then."

I hung up and started to holler for Pepper but when I looked up she was standing in the doorway. "Going out for lunch?"

"Yeah, with Miss Blumfeld. She wants to file a missing persons report and I don't think it's a good idea right now. Or better put, I don't think it would do much good."

"Well, since you're going to be enjoying lunch with a nice sounding woman, I'd like to take an extra hour or so and do some Christmas shopping. Get some little thing for Bo."

I grinned. “I thought you already had some little thing for Bo.”

“Max!”

Still grinning, I said, “Sure, do some shopping. Switch the phone to the answering service. I’m going to leave early anyway. I want to walk around the Port Of Entry area for a bit. I doubt it’ll turn up anything but at least I’ll be familiar with the area. Oh, that reminds me . . . An old beat cop nearing retirement did some footwork for us Saturday. Talked with some porters and cab drivers at the P.O.E. and looked the area over, so he’s on the payroll. I think he spent about four hours there. If it was more, pay him for his time when you make out checks Friday, but if less, pay him for four. His name is Murphy, and if you talk with him or he comes in, find out what his first name is. In all the years I’ve known him, I never caught his first name.”

“Did he turn up anything worthwhile?”

“Maybe. The taxi Bennett got into was a Checker, alright, but didn’t look right to the porter. He couldn’t read the company name. And she got into the taxi with a man who the porter described as a prick. Well, in so many words.”

“Prick sums it up well.”

“I thought so. What are you going to get Bo?”

“Not sure. Maybe a couple flannel shirts and some bubble bath.”

“Bubble bath? I never would have guessed.”

“There a lot about Bo you wouldn’t guess.”

“Could be, but I have a vivid imagination.”

“Even your imagination couldn’t keep up.”

I looked at her for a few seconds. “Maybe not, but some of the images I conjure up add a bit of spice to my life.”

“Get your own spice, Smilin’ Jack.”

I laughed. “Maybe I will. I’m going to stop by the tobacco shop, go to the POE, and then to Miss Blumfeld’s place. Should be back by three or three-thirty, give or take.”

“The afternoon edition of the Post will hit the streets between twelve and one. What should I tell Smith and Smith if they call?”

“Hmmm . . . hadn’t thought of that. Tell them to phone back after four. I’ll make a point of being back before then.”

“Okay, boss. Have fun.”

“I’ll try.”

Almost as an afterthought, I took the “nude” cigarette case from the safe and put it in my coat pocket. I was undecided as to whether I’d show it to Ari but is a reason arose, at least I’d have it with me.

I decided to reverse course and go to the Brooklyn port first and then stop by the tobacconists before going to Ari’s place. It just made more sense because the tobacco store was on Livonia near Jake Resnik’s photo shop and on the way to Ari’s.

Most of the bigger passenger ships docked at the New York Passenger Ship Terminal in Manhattan but the De Grasse had docked at Brooklyn Pier 12. The Manhattan piers and terminal were new, having been built at the insistence of Mayor LaGuardia several years earlier to accommodate larger liners. It quickly became known a Luxury Liner Row for the big ships that docked there, Normandie and the Queen Mary just to name two.

The Manhattan dock area could actually be looked on as an extension of Hell's Kitchen, an area between 34th Street and 59th Street, from 8th Avenue to the Hudson River, and one tough neighborhood. It wasn't a slum but it was seedy, with rows of tenements, street after street, some of which had been built in the mid-1800s. And it was Irish. During Prohibition it was said there were more speakeasies than children in the Irish area. They were run by gangsters like Owney "the Killer" Madden, who, in midlife, associated with the notorious Mafia boss Lucky Luciano. Madden controlled bootleg liquor, nightclubs, taxicabs, laundries, and cigarette concessions. In 1923, he took over the Club Deluxe in Harlem from Jack Johnson, the great heavyweight champ and changed the name to the Cotton Club. But early on, everyone thought Owney was Irish because he took over the toughest Irish gang in Hell's Kitchen, the Gophers, by the time he was eighteen. In fact, he was born in Liverpool England.

The most prominent and brutal Irish gang prior to prohibition was the Gophers, and they even had a ladies auxiliary whose members were every bit as vicious as the men. One of the male members, a fellow with the moniker of One Lung Curran liked to please his girlfriend. When she complained she was cold, he walked out to the street, blackjacked the first cop he met, and stole his coat. The story is questionable however. Cops generally steered clear of Hell's Kitchen.

There are a few stories that are true and verifiable: The Landmark Tavern, which opened in 1868 at the corner of 11th Avenue and West 46th Street, was a speakeasy favored by George Raft, the Hollywood tough guy who grew up in Hell's Kitchen. The building at 330 West 45th Street is famous for one of history's most talked about vanishing acts. In 1930 Judge Joseph Crater stepped out of the restaurant, into a cab, and vanished. It's a mystery that's never been solved.

But Hell's Kitchen isn't where I was headed. The Brooklyn terminal, officially Red Hook Terminal Pier 12, was older and the piers shorter but still handled an equal or greater amount of traffic than Manhattan. I've never been to the Manhattan terminal but as a beat cop some years before, had occasion to visit the Brooklyn piers on one assignment or another.

I would have preferred the trolley, I like trolleys for some reason, but took a bus to Atlantic Avenue and transferred. Then took the Atlantic Avenue bus to Hicks Street, a couple blocks short of the terminal. There was no need to go to the terminal, I just wanted to get a feel for the area. I do that with some cases—wander around an area to get a sense of it. Investigators sometimes talk of intuition or gut feeling and I'm a believer, but I often think it's a case of subconsciously absorbing surroundings and happenings.

I walked north on Hicks looking at the buildings and warehouses, one-fourth of which appeared abandoned. I crossed State Street and continued another block before turning left toward the piers and terminal. Depressing.

Not only the dirty commercial area but the realization that if Sarah Bennett was here, she could be in any one of the twenty or more vacant buildings in a six square block area. Or her body could. That was more depressing. I guess I was hoping to see a Checker taxicab with no company identification or even Smith and Smith entering or leaving one of the vacant buildings, but it didn't happen.

I stopped at an iron railing and looked down on the loading area laid out between me and the two ships moored at the pier. Cargo was stacked all along the dock and both ships were being loaded. I couldn't make out their names but they were obviously freighters. The DeGrasse had probably left on her return voyage a couple days after she docked. A mighty ship had docked and dropped Sarah off to her fate. Strange thought.

Though misty, I could see Governor's Island about a half mile out in the entrance to the bay. It was originally named Nut Island by the Dutch who discovered it in the early 1600s because of the abundance of hickory, oak, and chestnut trees. The island sits in the Hudson River almost as a divider, with ships headed to the Manhattan Dock area going left and ships headed to the Brooklyn terminal sailing right. It's a small island with a varied history, but mostly as a military base during the American Revolution, the Civil war, and now with the advent of the war in Europe there are troops stationed there.

I stared at the bay for a couple minutes, but water and docks weren't getting me anywhere. I turned around and let my eyes play in a 180 degree arc from left to right. Nothing but seedy buildings and squalid apartments. It would take an army to go through them all and I was short on army. And there was nothing but gut feeling that told me she was still in the area. Hell, for all I knew, she could be in Jersey. I felt like shouting a long string of four letter words, but instead, I shrugged, fished in my pocket for my pipe, lit it, and started to walk back to the bus stop. As the briar warmed in my hand it felt good and I realized I was chilled. Time to go to the tobacco shop and then to Ari's place for lunch.

SEVENTEEN

I thought about stopping by to see Jake Resnick. But it was past noon by the time I got to the Brownsville area of Brooklyn so I went to the tobacco shop a half block away from Jake's place. It's a small store, warm, and filled with the aroma of cigars and pipe tobacco. The owner is Michael Doogan, a mick who is affectionately known as Mick. In his fifties, short, squat, red faced and with red hair, he's always ready with a smile and a joke, usually Irish.

The bell above the door tinkled as I walked in. Mick was at the side counter filling one of the pipe tobacco jars and turned to greet me.

"Ah, Mister Max, did you hear about the Feeney's?"

"No, Mick, I didn't." I don't know any Feeney's but knew it was a joke coming on.

"Well, Mrs. Feeney shouts to the Mister from the kitchen, is that you I hear spittin' in the vase on the mantel piece? And himself says, no, but I'm getting' closer all the time."

We both laughed as he set the jar down and came to the main counter in the center of the shop. "An' what can I be getting' for ya today, Lad?"

"Couple pouches of Edgeworth and a package of pipe cleaners should do it."

"Right ya are. Have you tried other tobaccos?"

"A couple. Prince Albert and Velvet. They seemed lighter than Edgeworth."

"Aye, they are. Have you tried Granger?"

"No. Is it like Edgeworth?"

"Yes and no. It's medium strength like Edgeworth but the cut is different. Not quite as sweet either. Might be a nice change for you from time to time."

"Okay, I'll try a pouch."

I paid and was headed out the door when he called after me.

"The Feeney's have another problem as well."

"What's that?"

"He says the walls in his flat are so thin that every time he asks his wife a question, he gets three different answers."

I figured I'd walk to Ari's and was still smiling as I walked down Livonia Avenue. The weather was chilly but clear and I had about twenty minutes to kill. Time enough to enjoy a bowl of tobacco, so I opened the pouch of Granger. Mick was right: longer pieces and looked as if it had been pressed together and then broken apart. It tasted good, though, and had a nice nutty aroma. I took my time walking up Hinsdale and emptied my pipe as I got to the front door of Ari's apartment building and rang the buzzer.

She must have been waiting because it was less than thirty seconds before the door opened and I was greeted with a smile.

"Hello, Max."

"Hello. Ari." I wanted to say, "Hello, delicious," but that would have left the wrong impression. Right for me but wrong for her. She was wearing a pale yellow knee length dress with blue piping around the low cut neck that showed off a string of small pearls. It also showed off a hint of cleavage. I wanted to take the hint but instead, I mentally told myself to behave. Lotta good that did. I followed her upstairs smelling just a trace of a delicate perfume I wasn't familiar with but liked, and catching a glimpse of a few inches of thigh above the knee. To say I was a wreck by the time we got to her apartment would have been an exaggeration but slightly befuddled wouldn't have been far off.

She took my coat and hat and as I settled in a chair in the living room she asked if I'd like coffee or something stronger. A bottle of bourbon and a straw would have been just right but I told her coffee would be fine.

She was back in a few minutes, set a cup and saucer in front of me and settled on the couch. "Do you really think it's such a bad idea to file a missing persons report with the police?"

I took a sip of coffee and set my cup down. "It's not really a bad idea, it's just that I don't think it will do much good, if any. Loads of people go missing every month and if the person is over twenty-one, the cops won't give any priority to it unless there's some suggestion of foul play or proof they were taken against their will, or even murdered." At the word, "murdered," she flinched.

"Murdered," she whispered. "You don't think . . ."

"No, I don't." I decided to be blunt. "At least not yet."

"Oh, God!" She put her face in her hands.

I got up, went around the coffee table and sat next to her. I took both her hands in mine and pulled them away from her face. A tear ran down her cheek from her right eye and I fished a folded handkerchief from my jacket pocket. Surprise! It was clean. I put it in her hand and she dabbed her eyes. I reached out and gently touched her cheek.

"Look, Ari, I'm going to tell you what I know or think I know. Sarah was carrying messages between scientists in Europe and the United States. Her art business may have been real but was also a cover. Those messages dealt primarily with nuclear physics, nuclear fission to be exact. This information is crucial to a number of scientists here who oppose the domination of Europe, and perhaps the world, by Hitler. To paraphrase the professor I met with, it's believed that a weapon, perhaps a bomb, of unimaginable force could be developed, and if developed by Germany first, the result would be catastrophic for the rest of the world. So you see, the information Sarah has, may or may not be important, but I suspect it is and German spies wouldn't want to see it delivered. Perhaps more importantly, they'd like to know what it is.

"So I believe she was kidnaped in order to get the information. Now, I don't know what you think of intuition, but I have a feeling she's still alive. Not only that, but I think she's still in New York, maybe in the Brooklyn dock area somewhere. I just came from there. I didn't learn anything but I refreshed my memory and got a feel for the place. I have an associate who was there on Saturday and managed to get some information. Sarah apparently got into a taxi with a man. She appeared to do that voluntarily. The porter who supplied the information said it was raining and it looked as though the man offered to share the taxi with her. Two things about that: the porter described the man as being nasty, at least to the porter, and the taxi wasn't marked plainly so we don't know what company it came from, or if it was a regular taxi. It was a Checker, we do know that."

She handed my handkerchief back. "But it's been days since she disappeared. If it's Nazis who took her, they surely would have forced the information from her by now. I can't imagine them expecting to get what they want simply by asking."

"I can't, either. I know Sarah Bennett is smart and well educated, but you're her friend. How would you describe her?"

She took a few seconds to think. "Analytical. Resourceful. From what I know of her as a friend and what she's told me about some of her trips abroad, she adjusts to changing situations quickly even if it's as simple as a change in schedule. She once told me she represented an American buyer and made a fair offer on a Constable while in London but the owner couldn't make up his mind to sell. She left for Paris the following morning, purchased a Constable and a Pissarro there, returned to London two days later and purchased the original Constable at a lower price. Shrewd is another word that would fit her as well."

"I hope so. Analytical, resourceful, and shrewd is what may keep her alive." Without thinking I reached in my pocket for my pipe and put it in my mouth but didn't fill and light it.

She smiled. "Light your pipe if you like. I like the aroma of a pipe but not cigarettes. They smell bitter . . . sour."

I filled my pipe with Edgeworth and lit it as she picked up her coffee cup and started for the kitchen.

"Would you like more coffee?"

"No, thank you."

I thought about that for a couple seconds, listened, set my pipe on the table, then picked up my cup and followed her to the kitchen. She was standing in front of the pot, crying again. I set my cup on the counter, put my hand on her shoulder and turned her toward me. She put her arms around my waist and her head on my chest. I just held her, not saying anything. I decided this wasn't the time to show her the cigarette case with Sarah's picture on it.

She tilted her head back. "I'm sorry."

"Don't be." I put my hand under her chin and kissed her very lightly on the lips.

Instead of stepping back she pressed her body against mine and returned the kiss with passion. I was not as much surprised by the kiss as by the feeling akin to a hot flame running through me from head to toe. I put my arm around her waist, pulled her tightly to me and could feel the heat of her thighs through her dress. After a few seconds she moved her hands to my chest and stepped back, blushing.

She turned to the coffee pot. "I'm embarrassed . . . I'm attracted to you, very much, but I didn't mean for that to happen."

I smiled. "I did. I've wanted to kiss you since the first time we met."

She chuckled. "Nothing backward about you, is there?"

"No one's ever mentioned it."

She smiled. "No, I suppose not."

She turned to the counter, pulled a tissue from a box, wiped her eyes and blew her nose. "I feel so foolish. Oh, not for the kiss, but for tears. It's just that Sarah and I have been friends for a long time and the thought of anyone harming her, or worse, has me upset."

I didn't make a move toward her. Not the time or place. "I understand your being upset. It's normal and reasonable, but I do believe we'll find her somehow, and soon."

"Soon?"

"A matter of days." Thinking of the ad in the personals for Smith and Smith, I continued. "I may have a line on two men who might be involved. I emphasize *might be,* but odds are probably ten to one they are. I'm hoping to make some contact with them in the next day or two. But right now I'd like to change the subject."

"To what?"

"I'm hungry."

She laughed. "Oops! I have lunch in the fridge. Prosciutto ham and cheddar on sourdough bread and a fruit salad. How's that sound?"

"With a lunch like that, I may never leave."

She started to say something, apparently thought better of it, and pointed to the kitchen table. "Have a seat, Mr. Grant. Lunch will be served immediately. More coffee?"

"Yes, Miss Blumfeld, that would be nice."

We both laughed.

Lunch was enjoyable. We steered away from the subject that had brought us together and instead talked a bit about ourselves, a getting to know you kind of conversation. She had been engaged several years ago but didn't marry and gave no reason. She wasn't seeing anyone now. I told her some of my ex-this-and-that history and how I happened to become an investigator and ended with the comment that it was the first job I truly enjoyed.

After lunch, we went back to the living room with our coffee, sat side by side on the couch, and I retrieved my pipe and lit it. Neither of us said anything for a few minutes, but I wanted to ask a question that had nagged me for a couple days. I was hesitant because I didn't want to spoil anything between us but still felt it had to be asked.

"Ari, the first time I was here, you said you disagreed with your brother's politics, that your brother was *very* German. What did you mean by that?"

She was quick. "You don't think he had anything to do with taking Sarah, do you?"

Her question told me more than she realized. I was thinking anything was possible, but I said, "No, no. Nothing like that. I'm just curious about you and your family. I'd like to meet him, that's all. I paused for a few seconds. "Look, Ari, I really like being with you and I think you feel the same. We enjoy each other's company . . ." I hesitated again. Even for an old goat who's been around a bit, I was embarrassed. "It may sound foolish just knowing you for such a short time, but I'm really attracted to you. And it's more than just a feeling of fondness."

She reached out, took my hand, and put it in her lap. "I know it sounds crazy because I hardly know you too, but something is happening between us and I like it. As far as my brother is concerned, he's always been proud of his German roots and even more-so now that Germany has become aggressive in Europe. He mentioned once that he might return to Germany to join the army but I think it was simply a pipe dream or wishful thinking. He did join the German-American Bundt last year and went to some training camp in upstate New York but nothing came of it, or at least he's still here in New York. When the Bundt held that big rally in Madison Square Garden in February of this year, he attended that. I know because he stopped by to see me and asked if I'd like to go. I told him no—pretty emphatically, in fact. We didn't get into an argument but came close. I may not be a practicing Jew but I've read and heard stories of how Jews that fall under Nazi occupation are sent to detention camps. I said something about it to him but he said it's all lies. He's only been back here once since then."

I played it light and squeezed her hand. "Well, he's young. Full of piss and vinegar. Young people often like causes and joining organizations. It makes them feel important. It's possible America will get involved. Hard to say, but if we do, your brother may change his mind."

"I hope so. I really hope so."

"I hate to say this, Ari, but I have to get going and I need to make a stop on my way. I also have enough to do back in my office to keep me busy till late evening so I think I'll flag down a taxi instead taking a bus and trolley."

At the front door as I was leaving, she put her hand on my arm. "About that kiss . . . I'd like to try that again."

We did. With passion. The air must have gotten heavy because we were both breathing hard and she was blushing slightly. “Max?” She hesitated, then, “Would you like to come over for a late dinner sometime?”

“Does that include breakfast? I’m sorry. There I go again, not being backward.”

She was blushing in earnest but lifted up on her toes and kissed me lightly on the lips. “Wouldn’t hurt to bring a toothbrush just in case.”

“I’ll remember. I’ll call you. Soon.”

“Soon.”

I was half way to Dumont on the way to Jake’s before I realized where I was. To say I was in love would be rushing things but there it was, nibbling on my emotions. With Sarah Bennett, my nude on the cigarette case, it was part joke, part serious, but with Ari it was different, a different, deeper feeling. Something that perhaps could become permanent. It was a good feeling. Then, a thought: “Permanent, maybe,” I mumbled to myself. “You’re still gun-shy, Max old boy. You’ve been there before. Ex-ex, remember?” On the other hand, I did have a brand new toothbrush.

Jake was sitting behind his desk lighting a pipe as I came through the door. He glanced up, and drew on his pipe a couple more times before blowing the match out.

“You here to play chess, Max? Too early for bourbon.”

“No chess. Just thought I’d stop by to tell you Ruben Stein had information on the nude on the cigarette case. In fact, he took the photograph.”

"Must have been some special reason. Ruben doesn't take pictures of nudes."

"That's what he said, but I guess it was a favor for a friend who wanted some advertising to draw in clients in Chicago. A one-time deal. At any rate, I got the woman's name from him. Not an alias, either. Her name is Sarah Bennett and she deals in art. Sorta."

"Sorta?"

I figured I owed Jake for steering me in the right direction so went on to give him the highlights of the case and what I knew so far. When I finished, he leaned back in his chair and put his pipe in the ashtray.

"Max, my friend, I think you may be in deep shit with this one."

"Yeah, that's what I think, but I'm hooked. I need to find out what happened to her and if she's still alive. If she's being held by some Nazi wannabes, I want to break her out."

"That's a job for the police."

"Maybe. I just got done telling someone the cops don't bother much with adults who go missing, particularly if it's only been a few days. If they had to chase after every person who disappears, they'd have to double the size of the force."

"I suppose you're right. Well, good luck. I think you'll need it."

"Yeah . . . I'd better get going. I told Pepper I'd be back by four."

He sat forward and opened the bottom drawer of his desk. "Before you go, I have something for you that I thought you might like."

He put a sack on the desk, opened it, and pulled out a tin of tobacco and a pipe. "The pipe is one of mine but I rarely smoke it. It's a very nice bent Peterson from Ireland that I've cleaned with bourbon. Should be a good smoke. The tobacco is Edgeworth but it's a rich, high grade that's been pressed and sliced. Just crumble up a slice and pack it in the pipe. I was going to give it to you next time we played chess but I think now is better."

"I don't know what to say, Jake, other than thank you. It's a beautiful pipe. Tell ya what. Next time I come here, I'll bring the bourbon."

He smiled. "It's a deal. And let me know what happens with the nude, will you?"

"I will, I promise."

EIGHTEEN

If she had calculated her days correctly, it was Monday, late afternoon Monday, and exactly a week since she'd arrived in New York. She'd begun faking a cough the previous day when Smith Number Two brought her lunch, another ham and swiss sandwich with pickle. If she ever got out of this mess, she swore she'd never eat another sandwich, and pickles were in doubt.

She coughed a couple times while Smith Number Two was in her cell but if he noticed, it wasn't apparent. Then again, he hadn't said a word since she laid eyes on him. Later, she made a practice of coughing occasionally near the door, thinking they might be within hearing distance, but it wasn't till evening when Smith Number One brought dinner that he actually noticed. She'd remained lying on her bed wrapped in a blanket instead of immediately going to the table. She coughed lightly. Interestingly enough, it wasn't fake. Her throat was dry and ticklish. Now, wouldn't that be hell, she thought, if I did come down with a cold, or worse, pneumonia. She coughed once more. Harder. Number One took notice.

"Are you not feeling well?"

"No. I have a cough and may be running a slight fever. It's this room. It's cold, damp, and the air is stale. I need to get out of here and walk."

"I'm afraid that's not possible, Miss Bennett."

"Tell that to the doctor when he has to come here to treat me for pneumonia. In fact, explaining this setup to a doctor would tax your imagination. I'd love to hear that story. And if I really do get sick and possibly die, your explanation to your boss would be even more interesting. You'd have a helluva time with that and the consequences for you wouldn't be pleasant, I'm sure."

He said nothing but stared at her for maybe twenty seconds, looked around the room, then turned to leave.

"Speaking of your boss, tell me again when he's due back."

He stopped but without turning around, said, "A few more days. Perhaps by the twenty-third."

"Oh, that'll be nice," she said sarcastically, "just in time for Christmas."

Number One shrugged and left.

"Bastard," she said quietly. He's either devoid of emotion, she thought, or he loves his job . . . or both. She went on thinking about him as she moved to the table. Devoid of emotion, yes, but she couldn't imagine he loved this job. She'd become a pain in the ass and suspected he might relish getting rid of her, however that happens. He seemed dedicated enough, though, so it was either the Fatherland or money, but in the end, it made little difference. Another thought struck her. She might be able to convince the man in charge of this fiasco that she's mercenary enough to work for them if the price was right. Chances of that were slim but it might buy her more time. Then again, time for what? She sure as hell couldn't get out of her cell on her own. But time was time, and while there's life, there's hope. Funny expression, that. She had life for now, but damned little hope.

Dinner was a surprise: a rich vegetable beef soup in a double wall paper container and two thick slices of bread with butter. There were even small packets of salt and pepper. A steel spoon had been included but no knife, so she spread the butter with the spoon before dipping into the soup. It tasted better than it looked and it was hot. That was also a surprise but it told her something. The double wall container was obviously from a deli and if the soup was still hot, the deli was nearby, maybe no more than a couple blocks away. That information didn't do her much good as far as escape was concerned but at least it told her she was being held in an area that was populated, or one where there were workers round the clock. That could mean she wasn't far from the dock area and the Brooklyn Terminal where she'd arrived. She had to convince Number One she needed some fresh air. Maybe she could attract the attention of someone outside the building she was being held in.

She finished eating and was considering if she could hide the spoon but set that idea aside. Baboons these guys might be but they weren't stupid. They'd check for it. She was surprised when the door opened and in walked Number One. Usually it was Number Two who picked up the tray after meals.

He walked over to her and without preamble, said, "In an hour, I will bring your coat and we will walk in the loading area for twenty minutes. We will leave the door open to air out this room."

He set a small tin on the table, picked up the tray and left.

She looked at the tin. It was Certified brand aspirin, a twelve pack, but when she opened it, it contained only four aspirin of five grains each. She smiled. Not taking any chances, are they? No matter, taking one was probably a good idea and she did so with the remainder of her tea.

It seemed like more than an hour before both the Smiths were back, but it probably wasn't. Number One came in while Number Two remained at the door. Without saying a word, Number One handed her coat to her, walked to the table and set a copy of the New York Times Magazine on it. He then took her by her right arm and walked her to the door. Once there, Number Two took her other arm. They were in a long gray corridor of perhaps a hundred feet that ended at a wall. As they walked, she counted four doors on the same side as her cell but none on the other side. When they got to the end of the corridor, she realized it was simply a T with corridors running right and left. The one to the right was short, maybe twenty feet. It led to a door with a window in it but the window had been painted black. They turned left and walked about the same distance till it ended at a door that was barred. Number One lifted the bar, opened the door and they stepped into a huge warehouse area more than half the size of a football field, with a high ceiling of at least thirty feet. Number One let go of her arm and nodded to Number Two who turned her loose as well, but with the same movement slipped an automatic from a holster beneath his coat. For a moment, she thought they meant to kill her.

Number One stepped slightly forward. "You may walk around this area at your own pace for a short time. We will follow along but I warn you, Miss Bennett, if you try to run or make any move to escape, Mr. Smith will shoot you."

She nodded and began walking around the perimeter at as brisk a pace as she could manage after being cooped up in her cell for days. It felt good to walk and she was grateful to Number One for allowing her to do so. It was a strange feeling, being grateful to her captors, but that's what she felt. She'd heard about such feelings held by captives when given a piece of bread, cigarette, or cup of coffee. There was a name for it but it escaped her.

By the time they got to the far end of the building she was certain it was an abandoned warehouse which made her ninety-nine percent sure they were in the dock area, confirming her earlier suspicion. The doors, in what must be the freight entrance of the building, were huge, big enough to drive a tractor and trailer into. A smaller door was set in each one. And there, just inside one of the huge doors, sat the Checker cab that had brought her here. Though convinced of it, she took a route that didn't lead near it. Not the time to press my luck, she thought. There were windows on both sides of the warehouse, but they were at least eight feet up on the walls, and the kind that could only be opened by one of those long wooden poles with metal fitting on the end. She saw no equipment at all, but to her left, there were wooden pallets stacked ten feet high against the wall. The dust on the floor was thick, and they left tracks in it as they walked. She had walked around the perimeter three times when Smith Number One walked up next to her.

"We will go back now."

She didn't argue but just nodded her head. Her legs were tired—something that might have been logical given her circumstance, but it still surprised her. She thought of herself as being a walker of some merit who had trekked through the countryside of several European countries as well as Scotland and England and had never felt fatigued.

She could hardly imagine being happy to get back to her table and chair but she was. As she removed her coat and sat, she looked at Number One who was standing at the door.

"Thank you for that. I'm grateful and feel better."

"I cannot promise you we will walk again tomorrow. Perhaps. Mr. Smith will bring you a cup of tea now. Tomorrow, he will bring you hot water to bathe." And with that, he picked up her coat and left.

She thought about the walk and ever so slight change in the behavior of Number One. It wasn't friendly—accommodating would be more appropriate. As meaningless as it seemed, reasons ran through her mind. Maybe he was beginning to like her. Love her? Nah, she rejected that. Maybe it was his nature to be friendly and the tough exterior was an act. She rejected that as well. Deep down she knew he was a hard bastard who had probably killed in the past and would in the future. She had no doubt that was true of Number Two. Or maybe, just maybe, he'd received orders from his controller to keep her in good health. That was more likely.

As worthless as the exercise seemed, she was considering some possible means of escape when Number Two came in with a small steel teapot of hot water, cup, and two tea bags. As he set them on the table, she said, "Thank you."

He said nothing, but just looked at her for a few seconds and she thought she read hatred in his eyes. Then he turned and left, closing the door with a bang. Staring at the door she mumbled aloud, "He'd kill me in a flash and not even blink."

NINETEEN

It was just past three-thirty when I got back to the office. Pepper was sitting at her desk having a piece of pie with coffee and looked up, smiling. "Yours is on your desk. Have it now or save it for later if you've already had dessert."

"Wipe that smirk off your face."

"Smirk? What smirk? People often have dessert after lunch."

"Well, you and Bo's definition of dessert might be different than mine."

"I doubt it. But it sounds like you missed out. It's cherry pie. You like cherries?"

"Your smirk is getting smirkier. And no, I prefer aged fruit."

"What the hell does that mean?"

"Figure it out. Any calls?"

"If you mean the Smiths, no. If you mean anyone else, no. Getting close to Christmas and folks hold off on divorces till after the holiday to drop the nickel. Shoplifters and pickpockets are probably having a field day, but that never gets to us. Keeps the cops busy, though."

"Grab your pie and coffee and come into my cave. I have an idea I want to run past you."

I hung up my coat and hat, sat down behind my desk and filled a pipe. In the taxi while coming back from my stop at Jake's after leaving Ari, I thought about my short stroll in the dock area. My thought then was it would take an army to check out all the abandoned warehouses and tenements but that might not be completely true. Given a full day of looking, a few guys might be able to cover most of the area and report back. What I needed was a few guys and I thought I might know where to get them.

She was half way to my desk when there was a knock at the front office door so she turned and walked back. There was a sign on the door that said *Walk In* but it was small, a couple inches below *Grunt Agency*, and was often missed by clients.

There was a murmur of voices for a few seconds and then she reappeared in my office doorway. “Herb Spencer from your Saturday night alley adventure is here.”

I got up, walked to the outer office and shook hands with Herb. “How you doing and how’s your granddaughter?”

“She fine, Mr. Grant. I paid back the twenty like you said and bought a few groceries. I been around but no work yet. You said you might could find something for me so I came here.”

“As it turns out, Herb, I have something for you: two day’s work at five dollars a day. If you find what I’m looking for on the first day, I’ll still pay you for two. Fair enough?”

Tha’s great Mr. Grant. When do I start?”

“Be here tomorrow morning at nine o’clock. I’ll give you the details then. You’ll probably have one or two fellows with you but you’ll be in charge. Okay?”

“Okay. I’ll give you a fair day’s work.”

“I know you will, Herb. See you tomorrow.”

After he left, Pepper came in and sat next to my desk. “That was the quickest hiring interview I’ve ever seen. I’m clueless. Want to fill me in?”

"Yeah. That's what I was going to tell you about when Herb showed up. But before I do that, I want you to make a note to call our sign painter to change the sign on the door to *Grant Investigations*, and make both the office lettering and *Walk In* larger than what's currently on there. Also order some new business cards with the *Grant Investigations* name. Next item of business . . ."

I picked up the paper that had been folded in the cigarette case and handed it to her. "We need two photographic copies of this made today. If the Smiths show up, I'll give them one of them."

"What about the other copy and original?"

"The original will go in the safe. Put the other copy under some papers in your desk drawer, or better yet, in one of those law or penal code books you have on your desk."

"Got it. Now, about hiring Herb."

"This evening, about seven o'clock, I'm going to the Bowery Mission to see if I can hire a few fellows for some day work. One, maybe two days. I'll split them into two groups, one led by Herb and the other by Murphy, to search the dock area near the Brooklyn Terminal for anything that may lead us to Sarah Bennett. They'll need to look for a closed or abandoned warehouse or tenement showing some sign of recent use and also for the Checker cab with no identification on it. I don't think down-and-outs will draw much attention. Murphy can dress the part. The other guys won't have to. We'll pay Murph the regular investigator rate. The others, except for Herb, we'll pay four dollars a day. If they find what we're looking for on the first day, we'll pay them two dollars extra but no second day's work."

"Sounds good, boss. Best plan so far."

"The only plan so far. We don't have a damn thing to go on and we've been at it for days. I'm shit full of gathering information that leads nowhere, Pepper. Gotta do something."

"Okay. I'll call the printer and then go have copies made."

She'd just sat down at her desk when the phone rang and a few seconds later she was in my doorway. "Slightly foreign accent. Smith, maybe?"

I picked up the phone. "Max Grant."

"Mr. Grant, this is Mr. Smith. Perhaps you remember me?" From the sound in the background I figured he was using a public payphonc, maybc in a tcrminal. Maybc on a pier.

"How could I forget? I take it you saw my notice in the personal column of one of the newspapers."

"Yes. You have something to tell me?"

"No. I have something to sell you. I have a photographic copy of a paper found on Mr. Moller that might be of interest to you. It has a lot of mathematical writing on it."

There was a long pause. I finally said, "Mr. Smith?"

"Yes, Mr. Grant, I would be interested in seeing the paper. When can I do that?"

"At five-thirty this evening. We close at five o'clock. I will be the only one here."

"What do you want in return for the paper?"

"We'll discuss that when you get here. Bring money."

"Can I trust you will be alone?"

"I give you my word. If that isn't enough, don't come. Five-thirty." And I hung up.

Pepper was still standing in the doorway. "You want me to get hold of Bo and have him come over about five?"

"Thank you, no. I doubt seriously if there will be any rough stuff. These guys aren't stupid. If they see me as a source of information that could be valuable to them, they won't want to take a chance of losing that source."

"You sure?"

"Yeah, sure."

"I'll get the copies made now. Be back in thirty minutes or so."

She'd only been gone about ten minutes when the phone rang again.

"Grant Investigations, Max Grant speaking."

"Max, it's Murph. I just called to see if you need me tomorrow."

"Sure do, Murph. Can you be here by nine o'clock?"

"Earlier if you say so."

"No, nine is fine. I want you to take a couple guys with you and cover the dock area you were in the other day. Look for anything unusual as you did before. I'll supply the guys for you, but you'll be in charge. Skip going to the terminal again and concentrate on abandoned warehouses and tenements. See if you can spot the taxi used to take Bennett away. There'll be a second small group doing the same thing but north of the area you'll cover. Oh, and listen, wear old clothes. Nothing that will attract attention."

"I will. You know something, Max?"

"What?"

"I'm enjoying this. If you need me for other work later on . . ."

"Don't worry. I'm sure I'll have things for you to do from time to time and not busy work, either."

"Thanks, Max."

"See you tomorrow."

I finally got to my pie but my coffee was cold. I decided to make a fresh pot and while it was brewing, I lit my pipe and thought about the case. What I'd told Pepper was right. For all the running around, we still had nothing solid to go on. If something didn't turn up tomorrow or the next day, the only option I saw was to go to the police with all the information I had, and I didn't want to do that for a couple of reasons, one personal: It would mean I'd failed. Second, my ass would be in a heap of trouble for withholding evidence. DA Smith would love it. Even if I weren't charged and tossed in the can, he'd see to it my license was pulled. Not a good thing by any stretch.

I finished the pipe and was sipping fresh coffee when Pepper came back with the copies. They were good. Crisp and clear. She picked up a book on her way into my office, folded one copy and placed it in the book. It was a thick volume titled, *Law of Arrest Under the New York Penal Law and Criminal Code and Greater New York Charter.*

I grinned. "Yep, nobody would look for it there, not even the DA. Oh, by the way, you owe me a lunch on our Smiths bet."

"Okay. If you're still alive by tomorrow, I'll take you to the deli instead of having it delivered."

"Hell! I was thinking of the Stork Club on 53rd Street."

"Yeah, when you double my salary, boss, when you double my salary."

"Speaking of salary, cash flow, and other good financial things, I'd better phone Professor Fielding and give him an update, such as it is."

I didn't catch him at his office but was told he was ill and at home. The secretary gave me his home number and I dialed. He finally picked up on the sixth or seventh ring. He certainly sounded bad and excused himself several times during the conversation to sneeze, blow, or cough. I put as positive a spin on the situation as I could without giving the impression Sarah Bennett was sitting in my office enjoying a cup of coffee. I told him we had some solid leads, something I believed, and felt she was being held in the dock area near the Brooklyn Terminal by two men who may or may not be Nazi spies, but at least were Nazi sympathizers. I also told him we had a plan to find out where she was being held and hoped to have more information by tomorrow evening. I promised to phone him if we were successful. He asked if we did find where she was being held, if we would notify the police. I told him I'd thought about it and it would depend on the situation. If she was being held in a building that would be difficult to enter without a lot of force, we might need police. On the other hand, it might take more time than we had to bring them up to speed. Again, it would depend of the circumstance. We let it go at that. He thanked me and hung up.

The remainder of the afternoon was quiet and I was just giving serious consideration to sneaking into my bedroom for a nap when the phone rang. Pepper caught it and talked for a moment before coming into my office.

"It's an outfit called Fraley and Associates who want you to look into a fraud case, though it sounds more like theft. I told them we were pretty well booked, but they said they'd like to talk with you anyway."

"Okay, Pepper. Thanks." I picked up the phone.

"Max Grant speaking."

"Mr. Grant, this is Bud Fraley of Fraley and Associates. Your clerk tells me you're busy at the moment but we'd like you to look into a problem we have and are willing to pay well for it."

"Mr. Fraley, before we go any further, Paula Brown is a licensed associate of this office, not my clerk. And she spoke correctly when she said we were booked for the next week or so."

"My apologies. I assumed—"

I interrupted. "Some bad guys have made the same assumption and paid for it, but I'll tell her you apologize. Now, what sort of problem?" I winked at Pepper who was still standing in the doorway.

Fraley explained that one of their long time employees had disappeared and with him, a quantity of securities. About twenty thousand bucks in cashable securities to be exact, much like bearer bonds. The employee's name was

Arthur Schmidt and he'd been missing for a week.

"Have you informed the police?"

"Yes, but not till three days after he didn't show up at the office. It was then we discovered the securities were missing. We also notified the Securities Exchange Commission. We're not sure if or how the commission will handle this but the police, even though theft is involved, are essentially treating it as a missing person case for now. We need a more active investigation."

"I'll tell you what, Mr. Fraley, we can't assign more than one operative till Wednesday, December 27th but Miss Brown will make an appointment with you for tomorrow when you can give her all the pertinent information. I'll put her on the phone now. And Mr. Fraley . . ."

"Yes?"

"Treat her nicely. She's damned good and aside from that, she's licensed to carry a gun."

Grinning, I nodded to Pepper who returned to her office and picked up the phone. I thought the "assign more than one operative" line was a good one. It made it sound as if we had ten and overwhelmed with work. Ah well, lies by inference were sometimes necessary to survive.

She came back into my office in a few minutes. "I have an appointment with Mr. Fraley at ten o'clock tomorrow."

"Fine. Get as much personal information as you can on Schmidt. Talk with some of his coworkers. You know the routine. Does he have a wife, girlfriend, where he spends free time, vacations, does he like booze and does he frequent a particular bar, etcetera. I doubt it was a spur of the moment theft on his part.

Anyone who disappears with twenty grand of cashable paper doesn't act on an idea thought up while on a coffee break. And you might want to find out how well he got on with Fraley. That might tell us something."

I looked at my watch. "It's almost four-thirty. You may as well take off. You can beat Bo home and have his bubble bath ready."

"Good idea, boss. I'll be in it."

I groaned. "Get out of here."

TWENTY

After she left, I went to the safe, removed my .45 automatic, checked to see the magazine was full and a round in the chamber, and put it in my top desk drawer just forward of the photographic copy Pepper had made. I was packing my .38 in its shoulder holster. Both handguns raised my comfort level, but I didn't think I'd need either. The Smiths were after information and wouldn't want to do away with or piss off their source.

They arrived just before five-thirty, looked around Pepper's office as they moved through it to mine. As before, Smith Number One moved into my office while Number Two took up a position at the door. I was behind my desk.

No preamble. "You have information for me Mr. Grant?"

"You have money for me, Mr. Smith?"

"It will be determined by the information."

I moved back a few inches and started to open my desk drawer. Number Two snapped from his leaning position and put his hand inside his coat. I looked straight at him.

"Don't get your balls in an uproar, sweetheart, I'm just getting a photographic copy."

Number One nodded to Number two and he resumed his ten degree list to starboard against the wall. I took the copy from the drawer and handed it to Number One. He looked it over but from his expression, I suspect he didn't make any more from it than I had, but I could also see he liked it.

"How did you acquire this, Mr. Grant?"

"Friends in high places." Or low, I thought, depending on where Moller is now.

I picked up my pipe, struck a match, and put it to the bowl. "That was found on Moller's body. There may be more but I don't know yet."

"Where is the original document?"

"I couldn't get the original."

"How much?"

"Five hundred."

"Too much. Maybe we just take it."

"Fine. If there's more, you'll never know."

"One hundred."

"I'm easy. Two hundred and it's yours." What the hell, I thought, free money. And aside from that, money to pay for what I had in mind the following day. If the Smiths were holding Sarah Bennett, it would be a twist of fate if it was their own money used to find her.

He reached inside his coat, took out a manila envelope, pulled a stack of bills from it and counted out two hundred in tens and twenties on my desk.

I stood, picked up the money and put it in the desk drawer without recounting it. They turned to leave and I followed. Number One paused in the center of Pepper's office.

"If you come by more information, you will put ad in the newspaper?"

"Yes."

Number Two was standing in the hall doorway facing us. As Number One turned to leave I stepped quickly past him and said, "One more thing."

The punch I threw smacked Number Two square on the chin and caught him completely off guard. He literally flew out the door, slammed against the hallway wall and slid to a sitting position. All I said, was, "I owed you."

Smith Number One looked at me, smiled, then helped his partner to a standing position. "We will meet again, Mr. Grant, one way or another."

I stood in the doorway, watched them walk down the hall to the stairs, then closed and locked the door. I didn't want them coming back in a few minutes unannounced, though I thought the chance of that was slim. And I had no intention of following them or having them followed, even if I had someone around to do that. They'd be on the lookout and would lead any tail round the maypole. No sense putting them on their guard.

My stash cabinet was beckoning to me so I poured myself a double-double of rye and tossed it down. My pack of Lucky Strikes were also calling my name so I slid one out of the pack and lit it. It was okay, but by now I'd been spoiled by my pipes. It was then I remembered the pipe Jake had given to me. I took it and the tin of tobacco from my coat pocket and opened the tin. Jake was right. It was a rich, slightly sweet smelling tobacco in thin slices. I peeled off a slice, crumbled it, and filled the pipe before putting it back in my coat pocket. Checking my wallet, I found forty bucks in ones and fives. Plenty. After looking to see that nothing was lying about that shouldn't be, I stubbed out the Lucky in the ashtray, closed up the office and headed for the lower east side of Manhattan and the Bowery.

The weather wasn't mild but the temperature had risen to the high thirties and there'd been no rain for the day. The mid-weight overcoat I wore seemed more than enough.

Bowery Mission is located at 227 Bowery Street between Rivington and Stanton Streets with the El running overhead that drowned out conversation every few minutes as trains passed above. I got off the trolley at the short end and walked the block or so to the mission passing dozens of derelicts on the way, some standing, some sitting, and some curled up in doorways. There was what those familiar with the Bowery called "a curious etiquette" observed by those curled and sleeping. They often had a wide mouth bottle near their head. In the middle of the night, if they had to relieve themselves, they'd piss in the bottle and empty it down one of the sewer drains in the morning. Personally, I doubted if it was a display of good manners. It was more like common sense. Why get up in the middle of the night and walk half a block or more just to piss on a grate? If you did, there was always a chance someone else would take your sleeping place.

The street was sometimes called skid row, but that was a misnomer in a sense. These down and outs had skidded as far as they were going to go. For most, there was no further downhill slide except into a casket. Most were men, though there was an occasional woman to be seen on the streets. Booze played a big part for many but not all. The biggest culprit was no work. I was touched for a dime several times as

I walked and soon exhausted the couple bucks in change I had in my pocket. Some of the men said thanks, most said nothing. Strange, the things you notice. Their hands were always dirty and the occasional glance you got was not menacing, but more like an accusation—you have money and I don't.

I passed a tattoo parlor, a shop with guns for sale, and the Best Hotel at 94 Bowery advertising beds for 20 cents a night. The Blossom Restaurant at 103 advertised 2 eggs and coffee for 20 cents, a bowl of meatballs and beans for a dime and 3 large pork chops for 30 cents. Next door, a barber shop offered haircuts for 20 cents and a shave for a dime. A couple doors down a tobacconist displayed a sign in the window for Brown's Mule chewing tobacco at 5 cents a cut and cigarettes sold by each at a penny apiece. It was a no-hope neighborhood populated by those who had lost all hope. But as someone once said, the Bowery doesn't think of itself as lost. It meets its problems in its own way with plenty of gin mills, flophouses, indifference, and always at the end of the line, Bellevue.

The mission tried to inspire some optimism and confidence with talk, a bath, and a decent meal, but for most of the forlorn souls who lived here, despair was the watchword. However, I needed four to six guys and in the Bowery they'd come cheap. Well, cheap is relative. Four bucks a day to a guy with only twenty cents in his pocket is a pretty fair wage.

At the mission, I walked past a line of men waiting to get in for a meal. The line was short because they'd been serving for a couple hours. Inside, I found one of the assistants and introduced myself. He gave his name as John, no last name, but that wasn't uncommon. He took me to another fellow also named John, and I was beginning to wonder if the Smith and Smith routine had caught on in the Bowery. But the second John was a Leader and had some supervisory capacity so I told him what I was looking for—that I needed six men but would settle for four, for two days. I showed my investigator's identification and said I'd pay four bucks a day and if I didn't need them the second day, they'd get two bucks for their trouble. Each would get an additional dollar tonight to insure they had bus or trolley fare in the morning. I went into enough detail that John could be sure there was nothing illegal involved. I also told him I didn't care what color they were, whcrc they were from, or if they were rummies, just so long as they showed up sober in the morning and stayed that way all day.

It took almost an hour but in the end, I had five men that looked able enough to handle a day's walking in the Brooklyn Terminal area. I gave them each a buck, one of my cards, and told them I'd expect them before nine o'clock the following morning. I also told them their job would only involve walking and they'd have a fellow with them who would supervise and lay out their routes. They'd get more information tomorrow. The surprise was that none were named John.

By the time I got back to Brooklyn it was almost nine o'clock. I thought about calling Ari, nixed it, thought again, stopped in a drugstore a couple blocks from my office to phone her. What the hell. All she could say is no. She answered on the third ring.

"Hello Ari, it's Max."

"Oh, hello Max. I was hoping you'd call."

I was hoping you were hoping, I thought, but didn't say it. Instead: "There have been a couple new developments and I thought I could tell you about them. I could be at your place in 30 minutes if it's not too late."

"No, not at all. I rarely go to bed before midnight and since Tuesdays are my regular day off, I don't have to go into work tomorrow."

"Great, I'll see you shortly."

I started to leave the drugstore, stopped, walked back one of the aisles and picked up a toothbrush. So now I had two new toothbrushes, but ya never know. I paid for it, walked out on the street, put it in my pocket and pulled out the pipe Jake had given to me. I was guessing but figured I had at least a five minute wait for a trolley. I was right, and the pipe and tobacco were great.

Ari had slipped on a coat and was waiting for me on the bottom step as I walked up to her building. That's usually a good sign, or at least I thought so. It was. I got a hug and she held my hand as we walked up the few steps to the front door. She opened it with her key and we climbed the steps to her floor side by side. The steps were narrow. It was a cozy climb.

She took my coat and hat and told me to make myself comfortable, which I did at one end of the couch. "Light your pipe if you like. The aroma is nice. Would you like coffee or tea, or

I have a very nice Chablis, a white wine from France and some cheese."

"I don't often drink wine but that sounds good. Let's have that." A glass of wine for me was a rarity and then it was usually plonk that could be had for two dollars a gallon. The exception had been that glass of wine I'd had with dinner a couple days earlier. She was back a few minutes later carrying a tray with two glasses, cheese and some crackers. She sat in the chair across from me as I took a sip of the wine. It was slightly chilled and delicious.

"I hope you like it," she said, "it's a Petit Château and doesn't have a pedigree but I think it's very good. I keep a bottle or two on hand."

"It's delicious. Slightly sweet and tart at the same time." I helped myself to some cheese and crackers. I hadn't realized I was hungry but after the first bite, could have eaten the south end of a north bound cow.

"I've been meaning to ask you," I said as I took another sip of wine, "where do you work?"

"Saks on Fifth Avenue. I'm a manager of one of the women's fashion departments."

"Sounds like a respectable and important job. Have you been there long?"

"Just over five years. I started as a stock clerk but my college degree opened doors and I was promoted quickly. Few women there have any college, let alone a degree. I guess they figured if I had the gumption to finish college I'd be a good employee. In fact, when Saks opened a store in Miami last year, I was offered a position there but turned it down. Even with all its foibles and craziness, I love the excitement of New York."

"I do, too. I've traveled a bit, was a cop for a few years, worked construction in the Midwest, bummed around for a while, but I always seem to somehow find my way back to the big city. I even attended college for a short time but was antsy and wanted to move on so I dropped out. Sometimes I regret it. Most often, I don't."

She took a sip of wine and smiled. "So now you're a private investigator. I have to be honest, it doesn't seem like a very reputable profession. Of course, all I know is hearsay and what I read, but most of what you do is pry into lives of people for a fee, isn't it?"

"Well, there is that," I admitted, "but divorce cases only represent about twenty-five percent of what I do. Like many PI's, I charge high fees for personal investigations but that allows me to take on jobs I prefer and enjoy. I investigate theft, insurance fraud, conduct background checks, and quite often work with defense attorneys on criminal cases. Working with defense attorneys is my personal favorite because it makes me feel worthwhile, but those investigations are less than half of the assignments we take."

"And you look for missing women."

"Yeah, I look for missing women—or at least one in particular."

"You said on the phone there were some new developments."

"There are." I filled her in about Smith and Smith, both visits to my office, and also the search operation set for tomorrow morning. I didn't say the suspected connection to the Smiths or the search was my last hope of finding Sarah Bennett but she must have read it in my voice.

She reached across the coffee table and put her hand on my arm. "And if nothing comes of it?"

"I don't know. I honest to God don't know." Exasperation showed in my voice. "I could drop everything I have in the lap of the police but it would put my ass in a sling. The least they'd do is revoke my license for withholding evidence of a crime, and at worst, I'd do some time." I laughed. "Maybe when I get out, you could use your pull and get me a job at Saks as a stock clerk."

She got up, walked around the coffee table, sat down next to me and put her hand on my leg just above the knee. "I don't think it will come to that. I have a feeling you'll find something that will lead you to Sarah and I think you'll find it tomorrow. Call it woman's intuition . . . Something else you can call woman's intuition is that I think you're a good man. I like you a lot, Mr. Max Grant."

And with that, we kissed. At first, gently, and then with rising passion. I slid sideways on the couch and she came with me till she was laying full length on top of me. All the moves were there but our clothes were in the way. I ran both hands up the back of her thighs to her buttocks and she pressed herself harder against me, moving slightly side to side under my hands. She stopped, pulled her face back a couple inches, and slightly out of breath, said, "I think we'd be more comfortable in the bedroom. It's at the end of the hallway, and the bathroom is on the left. I'll meet you in the bedroom in two minutes."

She got up, straightened her dress and walked down the hallway. I followed as far as the bathroom where I combed my hair, took off my clothes except for my shorts and went to her bedroom where the door was slightly ajar. She was in bed with a quilt pulled up to just slightly over her breasts. I slipped out of my shorts and she raised the cover. I could smell the faint scent of her body and a light perfume.

"My God, woman, you smell luscious."

"You smell like pipe and I love it."

We kissed again, and again with passion and fire as we had in the living room. She responded, arching her body slightly and I moved downward, kissing one breast and then the other and continued moving downward, kissing gently as I did. She moaned and put her hands on the back of my head and I buried my face between her legs. After a moment, I began to move upward, kissing lightly as I did, pausing at her breasts, moving from one hard nipple to the other.

Then I was on top of her, hard and erect. I could feel her legs raise and lock around my body as I entered her. She whispered, "Max! Max! Yes Max," and we began to move, slowly at first, then faster as passion took us till we were thrusting against each other and reached that high point of ecstasy together.

We lay there, silent, not moving, till after a couple minutes I gently moved to her side and nuzzled her neck. That raised a "Hmmm . . . tickles," and a tilt of her head toward me.

I said, "I have an announcement to make."

"What's that?"

"I brought a toothbrush with me."

She giggled and I asked what was so funny. Smiling, she turned to me, kissed me lightly on the lips, and said, "I bought one for you when I was out earlier." We both laughed aloud.

The quilt had slipped to the bottom of the bed so she reached down and pulled it over us before asking if I'd like more wine.

"That sounds like a good idea."

"Good. You get it."

We both laughed again but I got out of bed, walked to the living room, picked up the glasses and then made a stop in the kitchen for the bottle. When I got back to the bedroom, she was sitting against the headboard with the quilt only to her waist. I set the bottle on the nightstand, handed a glass to her, sat on the edge of the bed, and noticed she was still smiling.

"Something else funny?"

"Yeah. You have a cute butt. It has dimples."

"We have something in common, then."

"Oh? What's that?"

"You have dimples on the inside of your knees."

She blushed, and then is a more serious voice, said, "I love being with you. I love making love with you." Her voice tapered off to silence for a few seconds and I didn't interrupt. "It's been a long time . . . I was engaged to a nice fellow three years ago but he was killed in an accident on 52nd Street and I haven't seen anyone since."

I thought for a moment about her choice of words. "A nice fellow? Were you in love with him?"

"You have a way of getting right to the heart of something, don't you?" She paused again. "I've thought about it since and to be honest, I don't know. He really was a nice man. Had a good job and I'm sure would have made a good husband and father if children came along. But there was no magic. Do you know what I mean?"

"Oh yes, I know. It was what we had a few moments ago."

She smiled. "Magic. Yes, it was magic." Setting her glass on the nightstand, she leaned forward, ran her hand slowly up my leg till it could go no farther and slowly began to message. She got the reaction we both wanted.

At midnight, we were sitting in the kitchen having hot cocoa. "I have to tell you, Ari, I think it's been more than twenty years since I've had cocoa and this is very good. I'll have to get some for the office."

"What time do you need to be there in the morning?"

"No later than eight o'clock. Listen, I've been thinking . . . Since you don't have to go into Saks tomorrow, why don't you come with me? I won't be going out with the two groups because if they stumble onto something important, they'll call me. If I were out looking as well, I'd miss out on being alerted to something that might need immediate attention. And it'll give you a chance to meet Pepper."

"Pepper?"

"My secretary and associate. She runs the office and most of the time, me as well. She's bright and has a great sense of humor. You'll like her."

"You don't have a . . . a sort of relationship with her, do you?"

I laughed. "No way. Two reasons: first, she wouldn't allow it, and for that matter, neither would I. And second, her live-in boyfriend, Bo, works the docks and is about the size of a mountain in the Adirondacks. If I made a move on Pepper, he'd tie me in a knot and drop me out the office window."

"In that case, I'd love to go. We'd better get to bed if you want to get up early. I'll set the alarm for five-thirty to give us both time for a bath. Wanna snuggle?"

"Yeah. Is that what you call it? Snuggle?"

We were both laughing on our way back to the bedroom.

TWENTY ONE

Five-thirty Tuesday morning came early. We woke, snuggled a bit but no fun and games. We took turns taking a bath. I thought about making it a twosome in the tub but knew that would lead to something more, and we wanted to be at my office by eight o'clock or earlier. I don't know why I thought it would be better for us to be there when Pepper came in than to come prancing in the door together after Pepper had arrived, but I did.

We got a break on the weather. It was cold but clear. The sky was pale blue without a cloud in sight. I hope it stays this way, I thought. Easier on the guys that are going to be wandering around the dock area this morning.

We arrived at my office at seven-forty, hung up our coats, and while Ari walked around the office looking, I put a pot of coffee on. We were sitting at my desk when Pepper walked in. She saw Ari and came straight through to my office, smiling. "New employee, boss?"

Ari stood and put out her hand. I made intros.

"Pepper, this is Ariella Blumfeld. Ari, this is Pepper. Pepper is actually Paula Brown but we don't tell anyone. It's a well-kept secret."

"Among other well-kept secrets around here," said Pepper. "Pleased to meet you."

"Pleased to meet you, too," said Ari. "Max was telling me about you last night."

Pepper raised an eyebrow and looked at me. "Last night, huh? Nothing good, I hope. I wouldn't want to ruin my reputation."

"He said you run the office and manage him as well."

"Yeah, well . . . the office mostly runs itself and Max? Sometimes he needs a keeper to steer him down the straight and narrow. You should apply for the job."

"I already have."

They were both laughing and I was embarrassed. "Alright, ladies, you can quit picking me apart at any time now. Pepper, we need that map of Brooklyn that shows the insert of the terminal area."

"Gotcha, boss." Still smiling, she walked back to her office.

Ari turned to me. "You don't happen to have a ladies room handy, do you?"

I pointed. "My cave is through that door. Bathroom is on your left."

I went to the safe and took out a cash envelope with some fives and ones in it, closed the safe and put the envelope in my desk drawer.

A moment later, Pepper came back with the map and whispered, "I take it you put a couple working girls out of business last night."

I leaned toward her and sniffed. "I take it you had a bubble bath with Bo this morning."

"You better believe it!"

"In that case, yes."

"Well, just so you know, I approve. She's very attractive and has a good sense of humor. I like her. Maybe we could double some night and you two could take Bo and me to one of those fancy places in Manhattan."

"Seriously . . . What you think means a lot to me, Pepper. Thank you. And yeah, when this mess is over, I'd love the four of us to go someplace nice for dinner."

Ari came out of my bedsitting room at the same time the men came into the outer office. Murph and Herb Spencer were in front followed by four men.

I shook hands with Murph and Herb and turned to the men. "I was expecting five from the mission."

One of the men stepped forward. "I'm Jake. Anthony couldn't make it. He's sick. Not hooch, he don't drink, but really sick. Running a fever most of the night and John told him to stay in bed." Jake held out a dollar. "He asked me to give this back to you."

I took the dollar. "Jake, when you come back here this afternoon, see me. Alright fellows, gather round the desk and take a look at this map of the dock area near the Brooklyn terminal. You're going to be in two teams. Murph here," I nodded in his direction, "will be in charge of one team." I put my hand on Herb's shoulder. "Herb will be in charge of the other. You're going to be looking for three people." I described Smith and Smith and Sarah Bennett. "There's a slim chance you'll see one or both of the Smiths but it's unlikely you'll see Miss Bennett. We believe she's being held against her will by someone. The Smiths are an educated guess. One thing in particular you should look for is a Checker cab with faded markings or maybe no markings identifying the company that owns it. Pay special attention to abandoned, stand-alone warehouses. Abandoned tenements are a possibility but unlikely because they're often inhabited by down-and-outs. I want to emphasize one thing: if you spot any of the three or the cab, don't approach them or it. Just amble on like you belong in the area and don't draw attention to yourself. Find your team leader and report what you've seen to him.

"I've marked out two sections on the map. Murph, you take the north section that starts just south of Brooklyn Heights at Atlantic and work south. Herb, you start in the south section just east of the terminal area at Sullivan and work north. You should walk the areas alone and not as a group. Plan to meet at a deli or diner for lunch. Herb and Murph will have money for your lunch. It should take about six hours to cover an area of six to eight blocks square in both directions. I don't expect you to finish up today but plan to be back here about four o'clock and you'll be paid for today's work then. If nothing turns up, you'll come back tomorrow. Murph, Herb, come into my office."

I took the envelope of cash from my desk drawer and gave them each a five and five ones. "That should cover any expenses including lunch and bus or trolley fare for each of your groups. If you need more tomorrow, or you spend more today, let me know. And something else: I think the people we're looking for, the ones who kidnapped Miss Bennett, are working for a foreign government and are probably Nazis. They're dangerous and probably won't hesitate to kill. I don't want you to pass this on to your men. I don't want to frighten them, but I don't think there's any danger if you keep a low profile. Anyway, keep tabs on your guys. Impress on them when you start that you don't want any trouble under any circumstances. Okay?"

They both nodded and turned to walk out. "Hold up a minute, Murph. I've been meaning to ask you what your full name is."

He smiled. "Hell, Max, I've been going by just Murphy for more than thirty years. That's what my wife called me as well."

"I won't spread it around. We just need it for our books."

He was having fun. "Now let's see, laddie . . . what the hell did my folks name me? Ah, yes . . . Daniel Patrick Murphy."

"Geez, Murph, no doubt about where your folks came from."

"None, lad. It was from Wicklow, just south of Dublin."

"Okay. Thanks. I'll tell Pepper and no one else."

After they'd gone, I turned to Ari. "Looks like it's going to be a long day for us and boring, too. If you want to go home or have some shopping you'd like to do—"

"Not right now. Maybe later this afternoon."

"Okay. There's a radio in my room. Turn it on and find some music you like. Make it loud enough that we can hear it in my office."

Ari refilled her coffee cup and headed for my cave. Pepper was putting some papers in her briefcase, looked up and winked. "I have that Fraley and Associates meeting this morning but I was thinking you could lock the door after I'm gone and make the time less boring for a while."

"Gawd almighty, Pepper, your one track mind is worse that my one track mind," I said, grinning. "Get out of here!"

"Just a thought, boss, just a thought. Oh, I have another. Maybe Ari would like to do some Christmas shopping this afternoon. If you were a nice boss, you'd let me have a couple hours off."

"More bubble bath?"

"Ya never know." She hollered toward my office. "Hey, Ari, want to do some shopping this afternoon? I should be back by one o'clock and we can have lunch."

Ari stepped into the doorway. "Yeah, I'd like that." She looked at me. "That okay with you?"

"Sure," I said, smiling. "I'd never hear the end of it around here if I said no."

I walked into my office, sat down at my desk and filled a pipe. I was putting a match to it when Ari came in and sat in the chair next to my desk.

"Are you always that easy going with Pepper?"

I took a couple puffs on the pipe and set it in the ashtray. "Let me explain it this way. She runs this office like clockwork and never hesitates to work extra hours if needed. I pay her a decent salary but we don't have overtime as such. If we handle a big case—by that, I mean one that pays well—I pay us both a bonus. If she wants to take some personal time for shopping, lunch with Bo, or some other reason and we're not under any pressure on a case, she should be able to do it."

She laughed. "Have any openings?"

I laughed as well. "Not at present, but you never know."

She put her hand on mine. "Do you think the men will find anything useful today?"

I thought for a minute before replying. “Honestly, Ari, I just don’t know. If nothing turns up today or tomorrow, I’m all out of ideas. But I have a feeling she’s being held in the dock area somewhere. We just need to find where.”

Herb phoned in at twenty after twelve. “Nuttin, Mr. Grant. No one that fits the description of the men and no women ’cept for a couple skaggy ones headed for the docks. We’re goin’ ta take a half hour or so for a bite to eat and then get back at it.”

“Thanks for calling, Herb. You can head back here about three-thirty.”

Pepper came back about ten minutes later, hung up her coat and scarf and came into my office. “We have a case, boss, signed contract and all. Mr. Fraley was very nice. One of the first things he asked me was if I really did carry a gun. I told him I did when I had to but didn’t think it was necessary for this appointment. I’m not sure, but he seemed relieved.

“Arthur Schmidt is pretty much a loner according to Fraley. A quiet guy who doesn’t mix much with other office staff. He’s unmarried and doesn’t date any coworker. But Fraley said he was a damned good employee. No sick days or time off for any reason except vacations in the years he’s been employed there. I talked with a couple of his coworkers and they said he hardly ever went out for lunch but usually brown-bagged it. The woman who has the desk next to his, a Mrs. Owens, said Schmidt took a two week vacation late last year and went to the southwest, or at least she assumed that because he had travel brochures for Arizona and New

Mexico on his desk. And she said he came back with quite a tan so he must have been outdoors wherever he went. When she asked him if he had a good time, all he said was yes, nothing more. I gathered up his calendar, planner, the southwest brochures, and some miscellaneous papers he had in his desk and will go through them later. Ya know, Max, if we do decide he went to the southwest, I'd be glad to go out there and look around."

"And take Bo and his bubble bath along for company, I suppose?"

"Nah, just Bo. I figure they sell bubble bath in Arizona."

"Bubble bath?" Ari had been listening.

"Inside joke," I replied. "Pepper can fill you in while you do some shopping." I turned back to Pepper. "Good job. You're in charge of the case. You'll have to do some interviewing but not till after tomorrow. Where did Schmidt live, by the way?"

"He had an apartment on Lexington Avenue just off 108th Street."

"You'll have to talk to neighbors and the building super. From the sound of it though, you might not get much. Did Fraley have any idea where he might have taken off to?"

"No. None."

"Okay. You may as well go shopping with Ari. So far, Herb's guys have struck out but I haven't heard from Murph yet. If I have to leave before you get back, I'll put a note on your desk. Have fun."

Daniel Patrick Murphy phoned at one o'clock. I just couldn't get over the name. It had a real Irish lilt to it.

"Nothing so far, Max. We're at a deli now and will have something to eat before going back out. It's clouding over some. Hope for our sake we don't have snow. Then again, it might be a blessing if we could spot tracks going in or out of one of the abandoned warehouses."

"Okay, Murph, thanks. Keep at it. You can start back to the office about three-thirty or so."

Twenty minutes later I was staring out the window, alternating between sips from a fresh cup of coffee and puffs on a pipe, when snow started to fall. Big white flakes. Not hard, but steady. At the rate it was falling, there'd be a couple inches on the ground in an hour. I wished I could get hold of the teams and tell them to stick it out an hour longer but unless they called in, there was no way. There was always tomorrow, but after that . . . I didn't want to go there. I thought about adding a bit of bourbon to my coffee but decided not to on the slim chance the guys would find something, anything, and I'd have to go out.

The girls came back just before three with snow on their babushkas and coats. They were laughing as they came in but stopped when they saw my somber face. Ari came over and put her arm through mine but it was Pepper who spoke first.

"Nothing?"

"Nope. Nothing. Herb called in before you left and Murph called about one, but neither team has turned up anything. They're due to start back in less than an hour. I guess we just wait."

TWENTY TWO

Emit Fielding didn't care much for meetings, particularly late afternoon meetings. Short meetings tended to be long and long meetings ran for an eternity. Professor von Neumann had promised this meeting would be short and Fielding hoped so. He was hungry, tired, and still trying to shake the cold or flu that had forced him to call in sick the previous day.

Instead of the meeting being held at the library, it was at the new building in a conference and work room adjoining von Neumann's office. Fielding was a few minutes early and happy to see a pitcher of water and glasses set out on a tray on the large oval table that dominated the room. And he could smell coffee. It was on a small table at the far end of the room. On a hotplate, actually, with another large metal pot that contained water for tea. He dismissed the water, headed for the coffee and was pouring a cup when John von Neumann entered followed by Doctor Einstein and a man he knew socially but had never worked with, Eugene Wigner.

Wigner, like von Neumann, was Hungarian and had been close friends with von Neumann since early school years. They both attended Technische Hochschule in Berlin and later coauthored several papers on mathematics. It was Wigner who prompted the meeting between Leo Szilard and Albert Einstein the previous

August. That meeting resulted in Einstein's letter to Roosevelt.

Fielding, coffee cup in hand, walked to the center of the room and shook hands with all three before they took seats at the table. He remained standing and asked if he could get coffee or tea for anyone. Einstein asked for tea, Wigner for coffee and von Neumann simply poured himself a glass of water. After returning to the table, he sat and looked toward von Neumann, assuming it was he who had called the meeting.

And von Neumann was quick off the mark, as usual. He had that reputation and it was often joked that in order to slow his lectures down, people would ask questions. He had a way of explaining an idea so quickly and clearly, those in the lecture hall would still be thinking about it when he was presenting the next.

"Well, Emit, any word on Sarah Bennett from your investigator?"

"Yes and no." Emit paused. "Please, it's not my intention to be vague, but from a short conversation with Mr. Grant last evening, it appears the situation is in a state of flux. He is convinced she was certainly kidnapped and is being held in one of the vacant buildings not far from the Brooklyn Terminal by Nazi sympathizers or spies. More likely spies. Being held—that is, if she is still alive. That's my conjecture, not his. He didn't say whether he believed she is still alive but he talks as though she is. He said he had a plan he would put in place today to find out where she is. He didn't go into detail but sounded confident."

"If he finds her, will he then contact the police?"

"He said it would depend on the situation. If it appeared it would require a lot of force, then he would. But he was concerned about the amount of time it would take for the police to respond. I had the impression he preferred to free her himself if at all possible."

Von Neumann thought about that for a few seconds. "Perhaps we should contact the police."

Fielding was rarely assertive but in this instance he felt he must be. Aside from that, he felt lousy and wanted to return home. "I think not. We reported her missing to the police days ago and were told adults go missing all the time. Unless we had some concrete indication of foul play, as they put it, they wouldn't look into it. Let me put it this way: We believe she's been kidnapped because she's carrying scientific information that may be valuable to us. We have no government standing. Our suspicions would hardly be enough to prompt the police to launch an all-out search. Mr. Grant, theorizing on what may be called intuition, in addition to information he's gathered, would appear to have the best chance of finding her."

Einstein, fishing in the large pockets of an ill-fitting sweater for what was probably his pipe, leaned forward and spoke in heavily accented English. "Never theorize before you have data. Invariably, you end up twisting facts to suit theories, instead of theories to suit facts."

Fielding smiled. "A quote of yours, Doctor?"

"It is not mine, I'm afraid. It belongs to Sherlock Holmes, but it is good advice."

"So, you read Sherlock Holmes?"

With a mischievous expression, Einstein replied, "Of course. Why should not one detective read another detective?"

Von Neumann shifted his chair to a slight angle. "Alright then, we'll wait to see what develops from Mr. Grant. Hopefully, it will be soon. Fielding, the only reason I wanted you here was to provide us with a firsthand account on the search Sarah Bennett. I know you're ill and appreciate you coming. You can leave if you like. We have a few other matters to discuss."

"Thank you. I will, but before I do, what information is it that Miss Bennett is carrying, either in her head or as notes?"

Von Neumann looked at Einstein and Wigner. Wigner nodded. "We believe she has up to date information on German efforts to move toward the creation of a nuclear bomb and Heisenberg's role in that effort. Perhaps more importantly for our endeavor, choosing the appropriate moderator for fission is critical to rapid development. As you know, the purpose of a moderator is to slowly prompt neutrons to thermal velocities by numerous collisions so that the neutrons are able to fission with U-235 and cause a self-sustaining reaction. We have reason to believe the Germans are using heavy water as a moderator. It has been suggested, perhaps by Bohr, that graphite could be a readily available substitute for heavy water. We believe Miss Bennett is carrying information that will allow us to move forward."

"I understand. Then it is critical that Mr. Grant is successful." Fielding looked directly at von Neumann. "He's promised to contact me this evening or tomorrow to report on his efforts. I'll call you as soon as I have any word. For now, I'm going home and going to bed."

TWENTY THREE

It was three-thirty and the teams were due to return soon. The girls had been back for almost an hour and I was filling my third pipe of the afternoon when the phone rang. I picked up.

"Mr. Grant? This is Herb. We may have something."

I sat up straight and put my pipe in the ashtray. "Go on."

"Well sir, it was Jake. We'd made plans cut off the search about three o'clock and meet at the deli where we had lunch. About twenty after, me and the other fellow—his name's Tom—were about ready to hoof it and let Jake come in on his own when he hustled in the door. He's here next to me. I'll put him on."

"Mr. Grant? It's me, Jake."

"Yeah, Jake, what've you got?" I was trying to keep excitement out of my voice.

"On the way to the deli, I was cutting through an alley alongside a vacant warehouse about four or five blocks from the terminal. When I got to the back end, I noticed some car tracks that disappeared through one of the big garage doors at the back of the building. They were car tracks for sure, not truck. I went back into the alley. There are windows in the side of the building about ten feet up but there were also crates stacked against the building so I climbed up to look inside. The panes are really dirty but I could just make out movement at the far end of the warehouse. There were two men and what I think was a woman walking between them. They had their backs to me and were going through a door at the far end. I spent about a minute looking at the inside of the place and then took off for the deli."

"You may be onto something, Jake. Great work! Anything else?"

"Yeah, sounds kinda funny but the floor on the inside of the warehouse is really dusty and dirty and I could see footprints that looked like several people had been walking in a big square just a few feet inside the walls. It was like something someone would do for exercise if they didn't want to go outside in the weather. Also, though I could barely see it, the car parked inside looked like a Checker cab. Couldn't tell for sure."

"I'm coming over there, Jake, what's the name of the deli?"

"Mitch's. It's on Union between Hicks and Columbia. The alley is about a block away just west of Henry Street between Sackett and Degraw."

"I'll find you. Tell Herb and Tom to stick around. I'll be there shortly."

Pepper and Ari were standing in the office doorway. "We have something and it sounds good. Jake spotted car tracks going into a warehouse and three people inside. Sounds like little to go on but he thinks one of the three was a woman."

I was out from behind my desk and putting on my coat. "Pepper, I'd appreciate it if you could stick around and pay off Murph's team when they come in. Give each man six bucks, not four, and tell them we won't need them tomorrow. Tell Murph to wait here till I get back or call. Maybe you'd better stick around for a while as well. Ari, honey, I hate to leave you to get home on your own, but I need to check this out."

"I understand. Don't worry about me, I'll catch a taxi. Call me when you can."

"I'll either call or come over late this evening. Promise."

Though the weight of my .38 should have told me it was in my shoulder rig, habit made me check to be sure. I debated packing my .45 Colt auto but decided against it for now. Even if warehouse turned out to be where they were holding Sarah Bennett, I didn't think we'd do anything about it tonight. I stashed my pipe and tobacco pouch in my pocket along with a box of matches from my desk and left.

I flagged a taxi as I got to the end of the block and settled in. "Mitch's deli on Union and there's a two dollar tip in it for you if you can set a speed record getting there."

He slammed the meter flag down with a, "Right you are, boss," and we were off. The streets were slushy and slick in spots but we slid there in a bit over twenty minutes. It was still snowing lightly as I paid him off and went into the deli. Herb, Tom, and Jake were sitting at a corner table drinking coffee. I bought a coffee and joined them.

I took my pipe from my pocket, filled and lit it. That whole process belied my excitement. I could tell the men were anxious so I nodded to Jake with a question. "How did you happen to check that particular building?"

"Herb told us to follow a pattern, to go up and down each block and that's what I did, but I knew it was getting late and I'd have to get back to the deli soon. Herb told us to meet here about three o'clock or so. I don't have no watch but I passed a secondhand shop and the clock in the window said five after three so instead of walking a new block I decided to finish the one I was on and then cut through the alley off Degraw just west of Henry Street. That's when I noticed the car tracks in the snow. They went up the alley and into an open loading yard behind a warehouse. Problem was, they wasn't no car in the yard. That's when I saw the tracks led to one of the large lift doors. I couldn't tell if the car had gone in or out and didn't know till I looked inside and saw it parked there."

"You said you thought one of the three people you saw was a woman. Is that right?"

"The more I think about it, the more I'm sure it was a woman. She was wearing a skirt or dress under her coat."

I took a sip of coffee, stood up, and pocketed my pipe. "Okay, Herb and Tom, you stay here. We'll get a cab when I get back. Jake, you take me to the warehouse." Before leaving the deli, I asked the woman behind the counter if she had a sheet of paper I could have and a pencil I could borrow. She tore off a square of wrapping paper and handed me a pencil from behind her ear. I thanked her and we left.

It was only a three or four minute walk but a slippery one. It was still snowing, light but steady, and it looked as though it might keep up all night. I talked while we walked.

"These guys, if they're the ones I'm looking for, are dangerous. Not only that, they know me. I doubt they'll be coming out in this kind of weather but you never know, so here's what I want you to do if they happen to come outside: Grab hold of me, spin me around so I'm not facing them, call me a drunk and kick me in the ass. I'll keep moving away and you can amble after me."

"You serious?"

"Damned serious. If they think I'm on to them, they may kill the woman."

"Jesus! Who are they?"

"Nazis or Nazi collaborators. The woman is an American scientist who is carrying information from scientists in Europe that's important to scientists here, and by extension, to our government. The other men don't know about this. Can I trust you not to say anything for a few days at least?"

"Yes!"

His reply was so emphatic, I knew he'd keep quiet. No matter how down and out some of us may be, we're a patriotic lot who loves our country.

We stopped at the head of the alley and could see the car tracks were by now no more than impressions. We followed the alley to the end of the building and the freight yard. No car had gone in or out for a while. We continued walking till we'd gone completely around the building. At the far corner on Degraw Street there was some light shining through what appeared to be a break in some heavy curtains at a small window but no other sign of life. Back in the alley, I climbed up on the crates and peered in a grimy window. The only light was from the high windows on the side I was at, and it was dim. I couldn't make out the tracks on the floor Jake had mentioned, but there was certainly a car parked inside at the far end and the silhouette told me it was a Checker. I climbed down and leaned against a crate.

"Jake, I need you to do something for me."

"You're the boss."

"Yeah, that may be, but I don't want to put you in a spot. I'll tell you what I want, and you tell me if you'll do it."

"Okay, shoot."

"I want you to walk through the freight yard to the door at the far end where the car went in. There's a small door in the large one and I'll bet ten grand it has a lock on it, probably a deadbolt, but I need to know for sure."

He took a step away. "Piece o' cake."

"No, wait. If someone comes out while you're there, play like you're a drunken bum looking for a place to sleep. They don't know you, but if it were me, it would be all over if one or both of them came out while I was there."

I watched from the corner of the building as he meandered across the yard walking in a staggered, broken line as some drunk might. When he reached the door, he lifted a canvas flap I hadn't seen, paused a few seconds, then started back in a broken line far outside the one he'd originally taken and kept up the act till he got back to me. While he was doing his drunk routine, I made a rough sketch of the building area and had just slipped it in my pocket when he got back.

"That was a great act, Jake. You would have fooled me or anyone else."

He chuckled. "Lots of practice. But I quit drinking about a year ago. There's a lock alright, a Schlage deadbolt. Pin tumbler. Looks new."

"If it's new, this kidnapping was planned in advance. It can be picked, then."

"Oh, yeah." He was smiling.

I was smiling, too. "I take it from that grin you know something about that."

"Yeah . . . well . . . once upon a time I was kinda handy with that sort of thing but I don't have no pick set no more. Sold it."

"I think I may know where to get one. What are you doing tomorrow evening?"

"Picking a lock, I guess."

"You're my kind of man, Jake, my kind of man. Let's go back to the deli."

We called a taxi from the deli and were back at the office in little over thirty minutes. Murphy was there but his crew had gone. Pepper was at her desk drinking a cup of coffee.

"I called a taxi for Ari. She wants you to phone her when you get a chance. And I made a fresh pot of coffee. Was the trip worth it?"

"Oh yeah! I think we may have found Bennett. All circumstantial but strong. While I'm thinking of it, take nine dollars out of petty cash and give it to Tom. Tom, you can leave after she pays you. Six dollars are for you and three for Anthony, the fellow who was sick and couldn't make it. I was going to have Jake give it to him but I need Jake here for a bit. Tell Anthony we're returning the dollar he sent back with Jake and the other two bucks are for being available."

Pepper set her cup down. “One more thing, Max. While you were out. Mr. Fraley phoned with a bit more information on the Arthur Schmidt disappearance. Fraley had a clerk go through all of Schmidt’s files and in one of them, she found a map of New Mexico with two small towns circled. Silver City and Jemez Springs. He said he’d send it over.”

“Might be worth a trip if Fraley will foot the bill. I’ve never been to the Southwest. A couple weeks out there and I might come back wearing boots, a cowboy hat and riding a horse up Flatbush Avenue.”

“Yeah, but you’re no competition for Tex Ritter. He can sing.”

While Pepper was taking care of Tom, I talked quietly with Murphy. “I’m going to try to break Sarah Bennett out tomorrow evening, Murph. You want in?”

“Oh hell yes! When and where?”

“I’ll lay it out in a few minutes.”

After Tom left I turned to Herb. “Herb, we’re going to try to bust some lady out of a warehouse tomorrow evening. Could get dicey. You want to help?”

“Whatcha mean by dicey?”

“Could be some shooting. Hope not, but could be.”

“Ain’t been shot at since the Great War. Didn’t like it then and doubt I’d like it now. But that didn’t stop me from shootin’ back and it wouldn’t stop me now. Count me in.”

“Okay. Jake has already volunteered. We have need of a locksmith and Jake has some experience in that profession. Well . . . experience of sorts.”

Murphy laughed. It sounded like a bark.

"Yeah, Murph, good guess. Just keep it to yourself." To the others I said, "Murph is a cop, a cop close to retirement. I'm licensed and so is Pepper. We can legitimately carry a firearm. The Sullivan Law says you can't own a handgun without a license and if you carry one without a license, it's a felony. I'm guessing, but neither of you have a license, do you?"

Both nodded no. "Well, what I have in mind for you should be safe enough. Jake will take care of the lock on the door we looked at today and then hoof it back to Herb. Herb, you'll be in the alley near the windows. Once Murph and I are inside, we'll need a minute to cross the open freight area to the door Jake saw the two men and a woman go into. I suspect there are offices and rooms in that section. When that minute is up, one of you throw a rock through one of the side windows, wait about twenty seconds and then bust another one. The noise should bring one or both of the men to the loading area where Murph and I will be waiting. If only one comes to check on the noise, we'll tie him up and go after the other one. If both show, we'll tie them both up and go after the woman. Sounds simple and straight forward enough that it should work."

Pepper spoke up. "I think you need a woman with you. Me."

I started to say no when Murph chimed in. "She's right, Max. If your Miss Bennett has been held captive for days, you don't know how she's been treated or what kind of physical shape she's in. May have been tortured or raped. Having a woman along might be helpful . . . a kindness, anyway."

They were right. "Yeah, makes sense. But Pepper, you'd better carry your automatic just in case things get a bit hairy."

"I plan to. What time tomorrow are we going to start the fun?"

"I've been thinking about that and need some input from you. It was about three o'clock when Jake saw them going through the door at the far end of the loading area. If they're allowing her to exercise every day, maybe it's at the same time. Then again, maybe not. I thought about breaking in about two or a little after and waiting for them to come out, but that could be a long wait or never. The advantage would be that we wouldn't have to break windows. The disadvantage would be that we'd have to stand right at the inside door because there's no place close to hide. More importantly, if we surprise them but give them a fraction of a chance, there may be shooting and Miss Bennett could be hurt. So . . . what do you think? Herb, Jake, you're in this too so speak up."

Murphy was the first to speak. "I think your first plan of creating a disturbance is a good one so it's only a question of when, isn't it? My vote is just before dusk, say about four-thirty or five o'clock. We don't want to turn the lights on in the freight area, assuming there is lighting. And it's possible there isn't any electricity to the freight area, anyway. That building has probably been vacant for a while. There may only be electricity hooked up for the offices. If we go in before five o'clock there will still be some outside light from the windows. Not a helluva lot but enough."

Jake and Herb were nodding their heads in agreement. I said, "Alright, we'll leave here in time to be in place by four-thirty. We can take a cab to the deli and walk from there. Murph, can you get hold of a couple pair of handcuffs and some tools to pick a lock?"

"No problem. I have to go into headquarters tomorrow morning but will take a half day off. I should be here about three o'clock. Anything else we need?"

I was filling my pipe but stopped because a thought struck me. "Just curious, Murph, but what's your opinion of Sergeant Belden?"

"Larry? He's a hardnosed bastard but a good cop. So far as I know, he's not on the take but won't turn down a meal or a drink if someone wants to buy. Hell, I wouldn't either when I was walking a beat. Why do you ask?"

"Curious. We've sometimes shared bits of street chatter or info from an informant if we knew it could be helpful to either of us. I was wondering if it would be wise to let him know what we're doing. What do you think?"

"Damn! I don't know. Let me get a cup of coffee and think about it."

He was back in two minutes. "You have some special reason to want to do that, Max?"

I laughed. "Well, it's a cover my ass thing. Assistant DA Smith doesn't like me and would love to have an excuse to pull my license, but he respects Belden's opinion. I was thinking if this little operation we have planned goes sour, it might be nice to have some unofficial cover. I wouldn't ask Belden to come with us but just fill him in on what we're planning to do and why."

"Well, it's a tough call. If you tell Belden, then he has to cover his ass as well if someone learns he knew about it and things go bad. On the other hand, you might need him. What it boils down to is if you think you can trust him, let him in on it."

"When you go in tomorrow morning, can you get hold of him and ask him to call me as soon as he can? Tell him it's important, no more. If you ask instead of me trying to connect with him, he'll probably call early. That reminds me. I have to make a couple phone calls in a few minutes. You may as well take off now. See you tomorrow."

I turned to Herb and Jake. "You guys can leave as well. Pepper, give 'em three bucks for a taxi and take a couple for your own taxi. You may as well travel in style." I grinned. "You can get home in time to run a bubble bath for Bo."

Murph stopped at the door. "Bubblebath?"

I winked at Pepper. "Inside joke. But if you ever meet Bo, don't mention it. He's bigger than both of us and works the docks. Being Irish, you'd call him a dock walloper."

"I ain't sayin' nuttin, laddie. Bye."

Two minutes later, I was alone in the office and headed for my stash cabinet. I poured a short shot of bourbon in my coffee, picked up the still newish Sasieni pipe, filled it with Edgeworth, walked to my desk and sat. It had been a tiring day but a profitable one.

I put a match to my pipe, took a few puffs while thinking of what I was going to say, set it in the ashtray and dialed. I spoke as soon as the phone was picked up.

"Professor Fielding?"

"Yes?"

"Max Grant. We have some very good developments but before I go into them I want your word you won't pass it on for twenty-four hours. Not a word to anyone."

"You have it."

"Okay. We are confident we know where Miss Bennett is being held and by whom. I've put together a team to free her tomorrow evening. Before you ask why we're waiting, it's because we just discovered her whereabouts this evening and getting her out safely will take some planning. In addition, the timing has to be right. The men holding her are dangerous and I'm certain they're armed. I don't want Miss Bennett or any of my people hurt."

"No, of course not. Are the men German?"

"Not sure. European at any rate. Either Nazis or paid conspirators. They're hard bastards, I know that."

"When can I let Professor von Neumann know?"

"You have two choices. You can let him know what I've just told you sometime after five o'clock tomorrow or you can wait till I call you later, probably around seven or eight."

"Might be better to wait."

"Yeah, that's what I'd suggest. One more thing: It's possible we'll run into trouble, maybe even likely. If we do, does your Princeton community have any clout with the New York police?"

"Considering the gravity of the situation and the likely foreign threat to our country, I'm sure we could bring some pressure if needed."

"It may be necessary. Hope not. I'll call you."

"Alright. Thank you."

I hung up, took a sip of coffee, and relit my pipe. I needed to call Ari but wanted to consider first whether I should go there for the night if she suggested it or beg off and stay home. Either way, I'd have to be in the office early in case Sergeant Belden phoned in the morning. After a few seconds I shrugged and picked up the phone.

"Hello?"

"Hi Ari. It's Max."

"Oh, I'm so glad you called. Did you find Sarah?"

"We think so but can't do anything about it tonight." I paused. Decision made on the fly. "Is it okay to come over to your place? I can tell you what happened today and what we plan to do tomorrow."

"Yes. I was hoping you'd want to do that. And . . . you left your toothbrush here."

I could hear the smile in her voice. It felt nice to be wanted. "I'll wrap things up here and be at your place in less than an hour. How's that?"

"That's fine, but I don't have much in for dinner unless you'd like some eggs and bacon. Or you could pick something up on your way."

"Eggs and bacon are great. I'll see you shortly."

I hung up, called for a taxi and was told it would be twenty minutes. Just enough time to rinse out the coffee pot and my cup and put a dopp kit together, maybe something I could leave at Ari's if the relationship develops into something permanent. So I tossed a razor, blades, a spare shaving brush and mug, deodorant, a bar of walnut scented soap and some toothpaste in the kit. As I was so recently reminded, I didn't need a toothbrush.

TWENTY FOUR

Today had been different for several reasons. First, when the Smiths took her for her exercise walk around the warehouse loading area she could have sworn she saw someone looking in one of the windows along the far wall. She just caught a glimpse of a man as they started through the door back to the office section of the building. She entertained hopes of it being someone looking for her but knew it was a foolhardy thought. Probably just a bum looking for a place to sleep for the night. No one was looking for her and even if they were, she felt it would be futile. Second was dinner. It was cold but delicious. A chicken breast and slaw with bread and butter. And a root beer. A root beer for God's sake! But it was a pleasant change from tea three or four times a day. It was a shame it wasn't a good British ale but as they say, "Don't look a gift horse . . ." What she wouldn't do for a scotch and soda. Hell, she might even trade the tongue of one of her boots for one. Nah, couldn't do that. The third difference was what she had heard in the hallway outside her door just before Smith Number One came in to tell her it was likely she'd meet with his boss tomorrow evening. She'd heard a couple people talking. Though Smith Number Two rarely talked, and never to her, this time there was a third voice, higher pitched and if she was not mistaken, a slight German accent. Though Number One didn't say it, she suspected it was a courier or messenger who had brought news that the Smith's controller was back in the country. And strangely enough, the third voice sounded vaguely familiar.

Then the thought struck her that tomorrow she might die. If the controller, who she was sure was the man who chloroformed her in the taxi, didn't get what he wanted, she was of no further value to him. He couldn't let her just walk out the door. Then she remembered the thought she'd had a couple days earlier. She might be able to convince the controller she'd work for them if the price was right, but in order to do that, she'd have to give them some information—makc up something plausible as though she'd memorized it. It had to be real but a mix of truth and fiction. And she had to have names—names that would be recognized, if not by the controller then by his superiors. And two came to mind: Bohr and Heisenberg. Niels Bohr was in Denmark, still a neutral country though she was convinced not for long. It was perhaps just a matter of months before Hitler's armies invaded. Werner Heisenberg, the German theoretical physicist who had been awarded the Nobel Prize in 1932 for his work in quantum mechanics, was in Germany and heading up a project in nuclear fission. Bohr and Heisenberg were old friends. She had been in both Germany and Denmark in recent months. What would be better than to say she had carried communication between the two? But it had to be something that rang of the truth, yet obscure enough to require checking.

Shc finishcd her dinner and was leaning back in her chair when she burped. A root beer burp. A small explosion. And that was it! She knew what she'd tell the controller. In the summer of 1939, Doctor Siegfried Flugge had published a paper in the German journal *The Natural Sciences* where he commented on chain reactions and the possibility of incredible explosive power that might be obtained through fission. To be even more convincing, she would use the German name for the publication: Die Naturwissenschaften. She would tell the controller that Heisenberg had queried Bohr about the possibility and how such a reaction might be approached.

She felt better now. At least it was a plan with some potential for success. A slim chance, maybe, but at least a chance. The only other thing that would have made the evening sparkle was a piece of cherry pie with a couple scoops of ice cream.

TWENTY FIVE

I was on edge. Concerned about what was planned for tomorrow, of course, but there was something else, that gnawing feeling in my gut that only happens for a couple reasons: either I'm damned hungry or whatever case I'm working on is going to go down the shitter in a hurry. I wasn't all that hungry. But we had a plan, one that should work. Just the jitters, I guess.

It had warmed a bit and the freezing drizzle carried only a few flakes of snow. In the back of the taxi I cracked the window an inch and lit my pipe.

The cabby turned his head slightly. "Nice aroma from that pipe. I used to smoke one at home but the old lady objected so I quit. Not a good idea to smoke in my cab either unless my passenger lights up."

I was looking out the window at umbrella covered people scurrying home or to a bar through the slush. "I like to smoke a pipe when I have some thinking to do." The cabby took the hint and didn't say anything more.

So what the hell was bothering me? Timing, maybe. They'd had Sarah Bennett for about ten days, plenty of time to wring information out of her. But if they had, there was no reason for her to be alive and yet she was, assuming it was her that Jake had seen walking between two men in the warehouse. Maybe we should have hit the warehouse tonight instead of waiting till tomorrow. I rejected that. Making a hurried attempt at night was foolish and would probably lead to disaster.

Okay, let's look at some scenarios: First, it isn't Bennett. In that case, we were going to make jackasses out of ourselves tomorrow and I'd probably lose my license. Second scenario: It's Bennett and she's cooperating. That would explain the length of time she's been missing and why she's still alive but given what I knew about her, it didn't add up. And third: Whoever was holding her, and I was convinced it was the Smiths, had held off getting rough for some reason. That made sense but the question is, why? Maybe it isn't the Smiths who are doing the questioning. Nah, that doesn't work either. Anyone versed in interrogation and free to use torture would have all they needed or a dead body in short order. Maybe, just maybe, the person who was going to question her wasn't immediately available. That fit, but unavailable to question an important courier for ten days? Hard to believe. Well, I'd put it all aside for a while and enjoy the rest of the evening with Ari. Maybe I'll dream a solution, that is, if I get any sleep. I smiled.

We pulled up in front of Ari's building, I paid off the cabby, tapped out the ash from my pipe and hit the buzzer for her apartment. She was at the door in less than a minute wearing a pale tangerine colored dress, silver cameo necklace with matching earrings and smelling of gardenia. That did it. I was done thinking of anything else for a while. I got a hug and kiss and she held onto my hand as we walked up the stairs. I didn't realize I was hungry till we walked into her apartment and I could smell bacon.

She took my coat and hat and looked at my dopp kit as I set it on the hall table.

"What's that?"

"Emergency suitcase."

She laughed. "Hungry?"

"Starved. I am now, at any rate. It's been hours since I've eaten anything."

"It'll be ready in a few minutes. Coffee?"

"Oh yeah!"

"I'll get it. The bacon's done. All I have to do is scramble some eggs."

She started toward the kitchen while I walked over to look at some pictures on the mantle above the gas fireplace. The fire was low but the heat felt good. I hadn't noticed the pictures before but then again, I thought with a smile, I was preoccupied. There were several, one of a less than middle age couple that I assumed were her parents and one of Ari and Sarah taken outdoors in summer. It looked recent, maybe in the past year. There was another of Ari and a young man who bore a faint resemblance to her. Probably her brother. He was medium height, light colored hair and with a faint clipped mustache. It also looked recent and had been taken outdoors in a park from the looks of it.

I was filling my pipe as she walked in with my coffee. "Eggs are on. Want to eat in the kitchen?"

"That's fine. It's comfortable and warm." I put my pipe in my jacket pocket and followed her, trying to decide which aroma I liked best:

bacon or gardenia. It was a tie—for now, at any rate.

We talked between mouthfuls of bacon, egg, toast and coffee. Hungry as I was, it tasted better than a steak at Delmonico's.

"I was looking at the photos you have on your mantle. The one on the left must be your parents."

"It is. Taken on a wedding anniversary trip to Wurzburg a year before they died. The others are me and Sarah last year, and my brother and I in Central Park in the fall of '38. In fact, had you come here a couple hours ago, you would have met him." She hesitated. "But you mightn't have enjoyed it. It wasn't a pleasant visit."

"Why is that?"

She hesitated again and I said, "If you don't want to talk about it, I understand. Relationships in families are sometimes not the best."

"Oh, I guess I don't mind talking about it. I mentioned once before we don't see eye to eye politically and today's visit was more of the same. He wanted to borrow four hundred dollars for a trip to Germany. I say borrow, but he's borrowed money in the past and never repaid it. I don't really mind so much if I have it. He could get a better job than he has, even in these hard times, if he tried. He has a good education but he spends all his time doing things for the Bund."

"Like what?"

"Organizing, running errands, passing out the tabloids they produce, things like that. He knows Sarah. Not well, but they know each other. They don't like each other, either."

"Why?"

"Sarah can be pretty blunt at times. She calls him a Nazi and a toy soldier among other things. Belittles him. For a while, I thought he was just infatuated with the German military and the Bund but now I'm not sure. He's serious about getting to Germany. He said he could do important work for the Fatherland and not in the army. Fatherland was his word, not mine. I equate the word with Hitler. Come to think of it, I suppose he does too. The Bund is arranging transportation, but he said he needed some extra money for daily expenses. I gave him a check for three hundred. I know it sounds terrible, but I'll be glad to see him go. He seems to become more radical every time I see him, and today we were both very angry. I was upset and told him Sarah was missing and all he said was, she did things to harm Germany and good riddance to the bitch."

I thought about that. I hadn't told Ari not to mention anything about Sarah to anyone, not that I'm sure it mattered much, but her brother's response was interesting. How would he know she did things to harm Germany? Maybe it was just a guess on his part based on her anti-Nazi remarks. Or maybe he was involved in some way with her kidnapping. I hoped not.

She picked up the plates and turned to the sink. "More coffee?"

"Better not. Can I help with dishes?"

"No, it'll only take me a few minutes. You go in the living room and light your pipe. I'll fix you a brandy."

I sat on the couch and filled my pipe. I was lighting it as she came in with a two small snifters a third full of an amber liquid and sat next to me. “It’s Armagnac from France. Like a cognac but not.”

I took a sip. “It’s delicious. Smooth with a subtle bite and very slightly sweet. I’ve never had it before.”

She smiled as she looked over the rim of her glass. “You’ve never had me before, either.”

“Seems like I’ve been missing a lot in life lately. And you sure are quick off the mark. Between you and Pepper, I’m getting beat to death.”

“You really like her, don’t you?”

“Yeah. She’s intelligent, quick, funny, runs the office like a well-oiled clock, and has a huge boyfriend. What more could a boss want?”

“I know what I want.”

“Now?”

“Now!”

We set our glasses on the table and headed for the bedroom. I made a short stop in the bathroom to use my toothbrush and take some clothes and equipment off. Handguns and shoulder holsters can get in the way of lovemaking.

She was just stepping out of her panties when I entered the bedroom. I moved behind and up against her, wrapped both arms around her waist and then moved my right hand down between her legs. Without saying a word, I nuzzled and kissed her neck. She turned, placed her hand between my legs and gently messaged. The reaction was immediate. She bit the lobe of my ear and whispered, “Mr. Grant, I think I’m getting a rise out of you.”

“Not a doubt in my mind, lady.”

We moved to the bed, tossed the covers back and fell, her on top and straddling me. I entered her and she jerked with a small spasm and moaned before leaning back, eyes closed. We moved together, slowly at first and then with rapidly increasing movement till we both hit the high note together. She held her breath for a moment, then trembled and fell slowly forward nestling her head at my neck. After a few seconds, she giggled.

I had to ask. “What’s so funny?”

“Nothing. Not a thing. I’m just so happy.”

Now granted, I’ve been around a bit, but that’s the first time a woman has ever laughed and said that to me after lovemaking. I chuckled. “I’m happy too.”

We lay close for a few minutes, then she slipped to my side, half buried her face in the pillow, and in a muffled voice said, “I’m hungry again. Would you like some fruitcake?”

“Fruitcake is only good with coffee.”

“Better with milk.”

“Really?”

“Yeah, come on, I’ll prove it.”

She got up, pulled a robe out of the closet, and headed toward the kitchen while I slipped on my underwear and headed for the bathroom for my pants.

The kitchen was warm, cozy. She’d lit the oven and cracked the door a couple inches. Slices of fruitcake, butter, and a couple glasses of milk were on the table. I spread some butter on a slice and took a bite along with a sip of milk. It was really tasty and I said so. "Delicious, Ari. How did you know I liked butter on fruitcake?"

"I didn't. I'm trying to butter you up."

"But you already did a few minutes ago."

We both laughed. It was pleasant sitting in the kitchen, late evening, sharing conversation and a bite with someone I cared deeply for. I've used the term *I'm in love* often enough but rarely in a serious way. This time was different. I was beginning to believe I was in love.

Ari must have sensed what I was thinking. With a subtle smile, she said, "Max, I think I'm falling in love with you . . . No, that's hedging it. I'm in love with you."

I reached out and put my hand on top of hers. "In addition to everything else, I think you can read minds. That's exactly what I was thinking. I love you, Ari. I don't know how that can be after such a short time, but it is. It's not only the love and love-making, it's the feeling of belonging."

"I know. It simply feels right. It's the rightest thing I've felt in years, maybe forever. Hmmm . . . is there such a word as rightest? No matter. There is now."

We were both smiling, both knowing. She took another sip of milk. "Do you want another slice of fruitcake?"

"No, I don't think so."

"In that case, let's finish our milk in the living room. You go ahead; I'll put this stuff away, make a short stop in the bathroom, and join you."

I'd left my pipe in the ashtray on the coffee table and lit it after I got comfortable on the couch. A few minutes later, Ari came in, kissed me lightly on the lips and sat in the chair across from me. She turned slightly, tucked her legs under her and said, "Now tell me what you've found out about Sarah. It seems we managed to ignore the subject since you came in."

So I told her everything: What Jake had found, his seeing a woman and two men enter a door inside the warehouse, and the plan to get Sarah out. I even included my concerns, not only about what we planned but also about the length of time Sarah had been held and yet seeming to be okay.

She was quiet for a moment, thinking. "Knowing Sarah as I do, I can tell you she hates Hitler and what he's doing in Europe. But she's smart. Cunning would be an appropriate word. It's possible she's feeding them bits of information, probably false, over time, stringing it out in hopes someone is looking for her. Could that be?"

"I considered that as a possibility, but if that's what she's been doing, she's strung it out for a long time. Sooner or later they'll get tired of it and assume they have enough, or maybe find that some of the information is wrong. I just hope I'm right about it being her in the warehouse so we can get her out tomorrow."

"And then what? Do you think she'll need to go to a hospital?"

"I hadn't thought of that but it's a concern. Pepper will go with us. She convinced me it would be smart to have a woman along, and she's right." I paused. "What do you think about bringing Sarah here if she's physically able? It would probably be after six in the evening and you'll be home."

"Good idea. I was going to suggest it. If she's alright, she could check into her hotel the following day or remain here for a couple. Whatever she's comfortable with. She could also contact the people at Princeton from here by phone."

I was quiet for a moment. Something had been banging around in the empty space between my ears for a while and as much as I disliked bringing the subject up, it needed to be out in the open. She could see I was thinking something through and didn't interrupt. I liked that. "Ari, you said earlier your brother commented that Sarah was a bitch and did things to harm Germany. Did he say what kind of things?"

"No, nothing specific, just that she harmed Germany." She put her feet on the floor and leaned forward. "What are you thinking?"

"In a sense, he's right. As a courier of scientific information to American scientists, she's doing what she can to damage the German war effort. The question is, how does he know?"

The light bulb came on. I could see the shock in her face. "Do you think he had something to do with kidnapping Sarah?"

"No, I don't. There's nothing that indicates his direct involvement. It was obvious to the porter at the terminal that Sarah didn't know the man who offered to share the cab and she knows your brother. Also, I'm convinced the two who are holding her are the Smiths. But the Smiths have to get instruction and orders from someone and I suspect there's no phone service hooked up in the warehouse. So unless they go to a pay phone, it means a runner is carrying messages back and forth. That could be your brother and would explain his comment."

She sat back, thinking. I didn't interrupt. Instead, I relit my pipe and did some thinking of my own. Here I was, at the beginning of a loving relationship that I may have just ruined. As they say, blood is thicker than water, or at least it usually is, and it was her brother we were talking about. What I feared most was the chance that he might be at the warehouse tomorrow evening and the possibility that he might be hurt when the action started.

She sat forward again and looked directly at me with a faint, perhaps perceptive smile. "That little idiot! If he's done something to harm Sarah, I'll break his damned neck!"

My relief must have shown because she continued. "I don't think he's a Nazi but he's neck deep in this Bund crap to the point where he's obsessed with Arianism, Fatherland, and Hitler. I'll bet anything they don't know he's a Jew, practicing or not. That's why he changed his name from Johan Blumfeld to John Vogel. Maybe if they found out, it would end this mania of his."

"I doubt it, Ari. And if he discovered you were the one who informed on him, he'd become enraged and take it out on you. If that happened, I'd be pissed." A funny thought occurred to me and I smiled. She saw it.

"What?"

"I'd be pissed enough to turn him over to Pepper's boyfriend, Bo. You'd get him back in a packing crate."

She laughed but the smile disappeared quickly. "Do you really think he's involved?"

"Yeah, but at a low level. I hope he isn't there tomorrow but if he's just carrying messages, chances are he won't be. We don't dare warn him not to be there because sure as hell, he'd run right to his handlers and that might lead to the immediate execution of Sarah. So if he happens to show up again, don't say anything about what we've planned."

"He got the money he came for so I may not see him before he leaves the country. May not even see him then. I don't know him anymore."

"I wish I could think of something positive to say but I can't. Sorry."

"Don't be. Not your fault . . . Max?"

"Yeah?"

"Stay the night?"

I smiled. "I brought my emergency suitcase. I guess I have to."

"Just cuddle. I want you to hold me."

"Cuddle. I like that."

TWENTY SIX

We cuddled at night, slept, and cuddled more in the morning, which lead to some passionate lovemaking. There's sex and then there's sex. Or perhaps better put, there's sex and then there's making love. I'm not good at definitions, but the emotions produced by either are worlds apart. Sex is a coupling, a release and little more. Making love is giving of yourself to your lover. And me? I was head over heels.

I arrived at my office ahead of Pepper at twenty till eight. The delivery boy from the deli was about two minutes behind me and since I'd only had toast and coffee at Ari's, a coffee and Danish were a treat. I put Pepper's on her desk and carried mine into my office. Munching, sipping, and occasionally pipe smoking seem to contribute to thinking so I took out the sketch I'd made of the warehouse and looked it over.

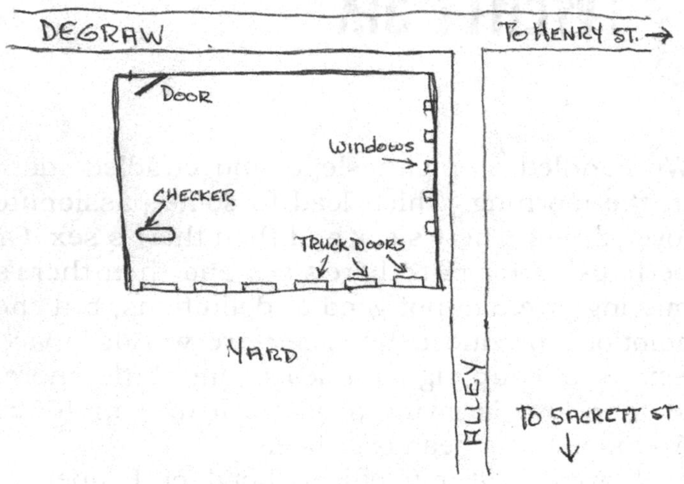

It sure as hell wasn't to scale, and I'd left out some things, but it was close enough. If that Checker cab was to scale it would be over thirty feet long. I didn't show the inside partition toward Degraw Street where the offices were, nor did I show the few windows on that side of the building. From what Jake said, the depth of the office area was forty feet or maybe a bit more. That could account for a hallway and maybe rooms on both sides of it. Risky. It was risky. One thing we might have in our favor was surprise. If we could get one or two of them to investigate the breaking of the windows, maybe we could convince one to act as guide. That might take some convincing but a .45 automatic is usually up to the task and I can be a nasty bastard if pressed.

Pepper came in with a, "Good morning, boss, just get in?"

"No, I've been here."

"Liar. You have that *satisfied lion* expression on your face. I know where you spent the night and it wasn't in your cave next to the office."

"Yeah, guess I have to fess up. I spent the night with Ari."

"Sure sounds like it's getting serious. I have something for you that will cement the deal. It's a present from Bo."

She held out a small paper sack. I opened it and lifted out a small jar of lavender scented bath crystals. I looked at the jar, looked at her and then looked back at the jar. I was at a loss for words.

"Bo says twenty minutes in the tub with that and you're irresistible. I can attest to that. In fact, if both of you spend twenty minutes in the lavender scented tub, neither one of you will show up for work the following day, so better hold off till a Saturday night."

I was smiling. "Thank you, Pepper, and thank Bo. Wait till I show Ari. Saturday night promises to be fun. What doesn't promise to be fun is tonight. Did you tell Bo?"

"Yes, but not in great detail. I tell him just about everything. He asked if I thought he should come along and I said no, that it was well planned. It is, isn't it?"

"As well as can be. We'll go over it this afternoon when the others get here."

"I was thinking about it on my way here. I think I should go into the warehouse with you."

"Surprise! I was thinking the same thing. I know I was reluctant to include you at first but I think a third armed person might make a difference, and I can't afford to give Jake or Herb a gun. It would put us all at risk. As it is, if someone gets shot, we'll have some explaining to do unless we can find a way around it."

The phone rang and Pepper caught it on the second ring. "Yes, he's in. Just a moment, please."

She pointed to the phone on my desk. "It's Sergeant Belden for you."

"Max Grant, Larry. Any way you can stop by my office this morning? It's important."

"How about I come over at nine o'clock?"

"Nine will be fine. See you then."

"Pepper was leaning against the door frame. "What's that all about? Or shouldn't I ask?"

"Belden and I have always gotten along reasonably well so I'm going to fill him in on everything we have and what we plan for tonight. If something goes drastically wrong and DA Smith gets wind of it, Belden just might be able to keep my ass out of the slammer. I don't know how he'd do it but he's a pretty sharp cop."

"So you're going to try to cover your ass . . . or our asses, as the case may be."

"You got it."

Belden was right on time and Pepper asked if he wanted coffee as she showed him into my office.

"Yeah. Thank you. Black'd be just fine."

I pointed to the seat beside my desk. "Have a seat. This is going to take a while."

He took a pack of Camels from his coat pocket, offered one to me which I declined, and lit up. "You in some kind of trouble?"

"Not yet, but I'm working on it."

Pepper brought his coffee as I went to the floor safe and took out the cigarette case with

Sarah Bennett's picture on it. I handed it to him.

He looked at it, looked at me, and said, "I'm in love."

I laughed. "You're the third person to say that."

"Who are the other two?"

"Me and Murphy."

"What's the story?"

"Remember the Danish guy named Moller who was killed in the alley just south of Johnny's bar? The guy's last words to me were to find the nude on the cigarette case. That case came from his coat. I took it."

He didn't say anything, just looked at me over the rim of his coffee cup, so I continued and told him everything. Everything from the paper inside the case, to Professor Fielding at Princeton, the Smiths, the guys I hired to look for Miss Bennett, to believing we found her, and to the part Murphy played. I added that I thought the guys who kidnapped her were Nazis, or at the very least, worked for the Germans.

When I paused to light my pipe, he took a drag on his cigarette and blew smoke toward the ceiling. He was still looking up when he said, "You've committed several misdemeanors and felonies, but you didn't ask me here to confess your sins, many as they may be." He was looking straight at me now. "I take it you haven't busted her out. When do you plan to do that?"

"Tonight."

He winced.

"Something wrong?"

"It's my bowling night."

"I'm not asking you to tag along."

"What are you asking, then?"

"To run as much interference as you can with the DA in case something goes belly up." I smiled. "Keep my jail time to thirty days instead of five years."

"I'm not sure what I could do if it goes bad other than put in a good word for you. I could say I knew you were working for Princeton on a case that required secrecy. That word, secrecy, seems to carry some weight these days. At least it would give them pause."

"That would help. Professor Fielding at Princeton assured me they could apply some pressure as well if they needed to. On the other hand, if all goes well, it could be a feather in your cap. You could say you coordinated the effort with me; that you didn't pass information up the line because of the firm stand I took on secrecy. It's known, even in the DA's office, that we've worked together from time to time, and I doubt they'd question you."

He thought about it for a minute while I puffed on my pipe. "Okay. I'll go along and keep my mouth shut till I hear from you. I have a home phone and I'll give you the number before I leave. You call me tonight sometime after eleven o'clock. That's an order, not a request. Now . . . tell me how you plan to pull this thing off."

So I told him. He listened closely and nodded his head a couple times. When I was finished, he said, "Should work as long as there's no more than three or four of the bastards there. One suggestion: get some wide surgical adhesive tape. If you manage to get these guys one at a time, you don't want them screaming their heads off. You put a strip over their mouth and then cover that with one that goes all the way around their head. Probably wouldn't hurt to blindfold them either."

I put my pipe in the ashtray. "Smart. Really smart. I hadn't thought of that. Thanks."

He scribbled his phone number on my note pad as he stood up. "I hope you pull it off but don't forget to call me either way. I'd better get back to the precinct and make my rounds. Pester Patrolman Howard."

"That reminds me, what's Howard's first name?"

"You ain't going to believe this, but it's Howard."

I laughed. "You know, somehow I knew that."

We shook hands and he left.

Pepper came in with a folder in her hand. "It's going on ten o'clock now and we don't have anything else happening till late this afternoon. Do you want me to do some follow up on the Fraley—Arthur Schmidt case?"

"No . . . Yes, come to think of it. You can check out his apartment area, talk with some neighbors and the building super if you can. You may as well have lunch on the expense account while you're at it. If you're not going to be back by early afternoon, call me."

"Oh, I don't imagine it will take more than a couple hours, maybe three. I'll be back before two o'clock."

After she left, I sat around for a while going over the plan for tonight. It seemed solid enough but in the back of my head, the old dictum of, *whatever can go wrong will go wrong*, kept banging around. I was restless, edgy, and decided to go for a walk so I called our answering service, slipped on my coat and hat, and headed out the door. It was cold but not uncomfortable outside. A weak sun was peeking through the thin, milky overcast but there was no rain or snow. It would be great if it held like this through this evening. The corner drug store had a soda fountain and a grill so I stopped in for a hot chocolate and a grilled cheese sandwich. The grilled cheese came with several slices of dill pickle and that got me to wondering why. Every place I've ever had a grilled cheese sandwich, it was served with pickle, usually dill. One of the imponderables of the universe, I guess.

A newspaper headline caught my eye as I was paying my bill so I bought it as well. Seems the Brits were finally giving Hitler tit for tat. British bombers shot down six German ME-110 fighters over Heligoland Bight in a major encounter. I finished my walk around the block, returned to the office, hung up my coat and hat, and called the answering service to tell them I was back. There weren't any messages so I decided to find out where Heligoland Bight was. We had a thin one volume world atlas on the shelf but it didn't list it in the index. I turned to the map of Germany and sure enough, right off the north German coast was Heligoland Bight, actually a huge bay, with an island or two in the North Sea, one named Heligoland. The article in the newspaper made a big issue out of the downing of a half dozen German fighters because they were known a Goering's newest destroyer aircraft. No mention was made of British losses.

Pepper came back about one-thirty. Apparently, Arthur Schmidt was one closed mouth s.o.b. who rarely talked with anyone. The super said that other than an occasional “good morning” or “good evening” he hadn’t spoken thirty words to him in the years he’d lived there. He did know about the vacation Schmidt had taken because Schmidt told him he’d be gone for a couple weeks, though he didn’t mention where he was going. Pepper asked about getting into the apartment but was told she couldn’t without a court order because the rent was paid through the end of the month. I told her to phone Fraley and see if he could work something with the Securities Exchange Commission so we could get in.

The rest of the afternoon was quiet but just before three o’clock I asked Pepper to put on a fresh pot of coffee. The guys arrived within a few minutes of each other at three o’clock. We gathered around my desk and went over the plan again. Herb would wait in the alley while Pepper, myself, and Murphy went with Jake to pick the lock. After the door was open, three of us would enter, Pepper taking up a position behind the front end of the Checker cab while Murph and I stationed ourselves outside the door to the offices. Jake would return to the alley with Herb, wait one minute and then heave a rock or brick through one of the windows at the Degraw Street end of the building. I couldn’t imagine the internal walls being all that thick and hopefully, the sound of breaking glass would bring someone into the garage area.

Murph had brought a pick set with him and gave it to Jake with the comment that they were only on loan. That got a laugh from everyone. Not having much experience at lock picking, I asked Jake how it was done.

His voice took on a professional, teaching tone. “This small L shaped piece is called a tension wrench. I’ll put the tension wrench with the longest side into the lock just at the point at the base of the opening where you would normally insert the key. I’ll use a half arrow pick and insert it into the lock above the tension wrench, working it gently to get the pins to set one at a time while keeping clockwise pressure on the lock with the tension wrench. Schlage is usually easier to pick with a hook but this half arrow pick will work fine.”

All I said was, “Okay, we’ll take your word for it,” and that got another laugh.

I turned to Pepper. “Call us a cab. Tell them we need it right away.”

I took a sip of coffee, picked my pipe up from the ashtray, checked to see it still had tobacco in it and lit it. “Well, guys, bundle up. We’re off and running.”

TWENTY SEVEN

Well, Miss Bennett, she thought, you may not live to see midnight. The day had been different right from the beginning. Her breakfast, if one could call it that, had been delivered by Smith Number One instead of Number Two, who had delivered it the past two days. She now knew Number Two as Helmut. She'd overheard his name used in a conversation the day before. Number One had been giving some instructions to Number Two and called him Helmut. Good German name, she thought.

This morning, Smith Number One brought her breakfast, and lately, that only happened when he had something to say. He did. His controller, or leader, or boss, was arriving today. She was never too sure what to call the man in charge and thought Number One wasn't all that sure either. He would be here to talk with her sometime late this afternoon, so there would be no walk in the open area of the warehouse. The second difference was breakfast. It consisted of tea, two slices of bread and one hardboiled egg. Not that she expected ham and hash browns, but it was a step down from meals she'd had in the past few days. She wondered why but thought it prudent not to ask.

Number One paused at the door before leaving. "I might suggest, Miss Bennett, that if you entertain thoughts of stalling or lying to my Haupt . . . leader, that you banish them from your mind. He can be brutal beyond your imagination."

He'd almost said Hauptmann. German. Captain, in English. She looked up at him from the cot. "You're going to kill me in any case. It makes no difference whether I tell the truth or lie."

"But it does. Quick and painless or long, lingering, depraved and painful."

He then left her to her thoughts and a lost appetite for eating anything. She did manage to get one slice of bread and the tea down but several times thought it was going to come back up. For what seemed like a half hour she stared at the bible on the table wondering if she could find solace there, but finally decided that even if she could, she wouldn't know where to begin to look.

She picked up one of the copies of the New York Times Sunday Magazine and began to leaf through it, not really seeing what was on each page. Toward the back of the paper, she stopped at an ad for an oven. It was half page and showed a woman in a house dress removing a roast, smiling, and getting ready to place it on a table where her husband and little daughter sat. Home, husband, children, bungalow, white picket fence . . . She had never given that sort of life much thought but now she longed for it; longed for the experience of it. She wasn't the type to cry, and didn't, but she felt a sense of forlorn sadness at the thought of missing the opportunity.

Reflections . . . reflections . . . She'd read somewhere that at the moment of violent death, a person's life flashed before their eyes.

Thoughts that came to her of her life were the same but in slow motion. She skipped past her early life—her childhood was uneventful, mundane. It was in high school she discovered her talent for two seemingly unrelated fields: mathematics and art. And though she didn't have a photographic memory as she'd implied to the Smiths, she had the ability to play mind-games that linked things together, and those things she could remember. Those links connected to images, connected to other links, connected to memory. She had no idea how or why it worked or why she had or developed the ability, but there it was.

And she used it. She graduated from City College New York near the top of her class and though her degree was not in mathematics, it was her second major. In some of her math and physics classes, she was the only woman in attendance. She applied for admission to The University of London and was accepted. That posed a problem, however. She hadn't enough money for boat fare plus living expenses in London for a couple months till she could find a job. Through a friend of a friend, she learned of a one or two day sitting, posing nude for a man who was preparing an exhibit for a Chicago show. He wanted to put pictures on handouts or trinkets that would attract attention. She took the job. She never saw the developed photos but learned from her friend later they were put on metal match-safes and cigarette cases. Most importantly, they paid for her passage and expenses for the first couple months in London.

She spent two years at University of London and received an advanced degree but not the

PhD in mathematics she had hoped for. But in those two years, she fell in love with England and the British Isles. She became a Rambler, as the Brits called those who took walking trips throughout England, Scotland and Wales. And if she loved England, she was passionate about the Cotswolds and the tiny villages of honey-colored limestone with thatched cottages. She had dreams of settling there one day.

She returned to the States and by a stroke of luck, managed to secure a position as an instructor in the math department at Princeton University. Two months later, she was shopping at Saks when, to her delight, she ran into Ariella Blumfeld who she hadn't seen since her days at City College. They had roomed together the last two semesters she was there and they enjoyed each other's company. For the last couple years in England, they'd stayed in touch with the occasional card or letter, but between her current duties at Princeton and getting settled in, she hadn't thought of contacting Ari. That changed immediately. It was as if no time at all had passed and from then on, they got together regularly for dinners, theater, or the occasional double date. But that changed early in 1939 when she took on the assignment that eventually put her in the mess she was in now.

In February of '39, she was approached by several members of the Institute for Advanced Study at Princeton and asked if she would take an assignment to Europe posing as an art dealer. Her expenses would be paid for out of a special fund and any profit made on her art dealings would be hers. In reality, she would be carrying information and messages between scientists, including several in Germany. Hitler was on the move, and open contacts between scientists in German controlled zones and America or England were severely limited. Germany had annexed Austria in March of '38 and in March of '39, had invaded Czechoslovakia. She made two trips, the first in April and the second one began in October. The first had been profitable both in art and information. The second? Well, this was the second.

At midday, Number One brought her a sandwich, a cup of tea, and something else. After he set the sandwich on the table he reached in his pocket and handed her watch to her with the comment, "I thought perhaps you would like your watch. Mr. Dresner will be here at approximately four o'clock."

"His name is Dresner, huh?"

"It is."

"German, if I'm not mistaken."

He paused, looked at her, opened his mouth as if to say something more but didn't. He just turned and walked out.

She put the watch on and looked at the time. Twelve-forty. She felt an emptiness but not one of hunger. She couldn't eat, at least not now. She covered the sandwich with a page she tore out of the Times magazine.

The day stumbled on, as did her thoughts. Thoughts that were random, no substance or sequence to them. At one point she though she should make peace with God but the next immediate thought—which one?—brought a smile to her face for the first time that day.

At ten minutes to four, she heard voices in the hallway. Five minutes later, Both Smiths and Dresner walked into her cell. A fourth man stood outside the door. She had been sitting on her bunk but stood and moved forward a few feet.

Dresner moved in front of her. "You remember me, I'm sure, Miss Bennett. I have an hour to waste on you, no more. We will talk."

She started to say, "Yes we will," when he slapped her with tremendous force, knocking her back three paces to fall onto the cot. The slap and immediate terror brought tears to her eyes. All she could think was—I won't last an hour.

TWENTY EIGHT

I've often thought college kids could probably pack twenty bodies in a Checker cab so the five of us were comfortable in back with Herb and Jake on jump seats. The cabbie must have thought it strange, given our destination in the dock area, but he didn't say anything.

We arrived at the deli about four-fifteen just as dusk was settling in. It was cold, thinly overcast, but no snow. We went in, took a couple tables and had coffee. No talking about the upcoming venture. A little after four-thirty I put a quarter on the table for a tip, nodded and stood. We walked to the corner of Sackett and the alley, and I went over again what we planned to do. Up front, the most important role belonged to Jake and Herb who would have to break some windows along the side. After that, they would become spectators.

When we came alongside the building, Jake climbed up on some stacked crates and peered in the window as he'd done the day before. After a minute, he was back on the ground.

"No movement inside but the Checker is there, parked where it was before, in line with the first garage door at the west end."

"Okay, folks," I said, "let's get started."

Herb stayed in the alley while the rest of us went through the freight yard to the second door from the west end. Jake pulled the picks from his pocket, inserted them in the door lock and worked his magic. It took all of twenty seconds and we were inside. Jake hoofed it back to the alley where Herb waited. Pepper took up her position on the garage door side of the Checker cab toward the front, gun in hand, leaning forward so she could only be seen head-on above the hood. Murph and I planted ourselves next to the hinges side of the door that went into the offices and rooms. When the door opened, it would hide us from anyone coming out. We'd been in position about ten seconds when a brick flew through one of the windows. Five seconds later another window blew in. Pressed against the wall, we waited. Then we heard footsteps that stopped just on the other side of the door. Whoever it was, must have been listening. At that moment, a large rock came flying through another window, blowing shards of glass twenty feet inside the warehouse.

The door flew open and a slim, slightly built man carrying a revolver took three steps into the garage before spotting Pepper, partially hidden, on the other side of the cab. I knew him from the picture on Ari's fireplace mantle. It was her brother and that put me in a bind. I didn't want him to see my face. The reasons were complex and of course had a lot to do with my relationship with Ari. As negatively as she'd spoken of him, he was still her brother. I didn't want to shoot him.

He leveled his revolver. "Come out from behind that cab!"

I took three steps, grabbed the back of his collar and at the same time jammed my .45 against the back of his head right at the top of his neck. In my best gravelly voice I said, "Don't move or I'll blow your fucking head off!"

He froze but tried turning his head. "Look straight ahead! Murph—tape."

Murph came up alongside of John Vogel, as he now called himself, relieved him of his revolver and handed it to me before taping his mouth and eyes. Then he handcuffed him, hands behind his back. The humorous thought suddenly struck me that removing the tape from his eyes would probably take his eyebrows with it. Murph walked him to the wall and sat him down against it with an admonition of, "Move and you get shot."

By this time, Pepper had joined us. We stepped through the door into a short hallway that was part of a T shaped corridor. We were in the top part of the T with a hallway running parallel to the front of the building off of it. With Murph and Pepper behind me, I stopped at the hallway intersection and listened before peeking around the corner. The corridor was a long one and I could barely hear the murmur of voices coming from the far end. I turned back to Pepper and Murph, and in a whisper, said, "Long hallway, maybe a hundred feet, and I think I hear voices at the far end. We'll have to hustle, but as quietly as possible. If we get caught in this open hallway, we're an easy target."

We were about half way down the hallway to the second room from the far end when we began to hear clearly. The door to the room was partially open and that's where the voices were coming from. The first voice I heard was a woman's, not crying, but plaintive. "I've told you everything I know and I made you an offer to get more. What more do you want?"

Smack! Even I winced.

"Listen up, bitch! I know you were carrying papers. Papers that dealt with moderators for nuclear fission. I want them! Now! Take your clothes off."

She murmured something. I couldn't make it out.

Then the man's voice: "Helmut, take her clothes off.

There was a scuffle and sound of ripping cloth. The man's voice again. "Turn her over and fuck her from behind."

Then muffled, "No . . . no . . . no . . ."

We almost made it when I heard a voice I'd heard before: Smith Number One. He came to the open door. "What's keeping John?"

Ten feet short. He stepped outside the door, saw me immediately, stopped and slapped his hand inside his coat. The sound of my .45 in that hallway was defining. The slug hit the edge of the doorframe, ricocheted, and hit him in the left side spinning him off balance. I slammed into him, my heavy automatic smashing into his forehead as we both fell into the room. Murph took a stance just inside the doorway with his service revolver pointed directly at the head of a tall man in suit and tie. Murph didn't say a word; he just cocked his revolver and smiled. The guy got the message. While I was picking myself up from Smith Number One who was unconscious, Pepper came around Murph, saw what was happening at the table against the wall and raised her .32 automatic. Smith Number Two, who we now knew as Helmut, was behind Sarah and still plugged in. He had turned his head and was looking over his shoulder when Pepper shot him in the ass. He screamed, fell to one side and down to the floor. Sarah never moved. Pepper grabbed a blanket off the cot, put it over and around Sarah and then turned her, wrapping her arms around her before setting her gently on the chair.

I was on my feet and walked over to Helmut. His pants were down around his ankles, and he had his hand on his ass. It was bloody. I kicked him in the face. Felt good. He screamed, so I kicked him again. He shut up.

I walked over to the guy in the suit that was being covered by Murph, spun him around and frisked him for a gun. None. I turned him around so he was facing me and gave him a shove. "Stand against the wall!"

He moved back till he came in contact with the front wall of the room. I asked, "What's your name?"

He stuttered, "St-St-Stephen Dresner. A-A-Are you going to kill me?"

"I haven't decided yet. Very slowly, take your wallet out and hand it to this man." I indicated Murph.

I walked over to Smith Number One who was still out, found his wallet in his inside coat pocket and handed it to Murph as well. I found Helmut's wallet in his coat on the cot and slipped it into my jacket pocket. Then I walked over to Pepper and Sarah. And yes, it was Sarah Bennett for sure. She was older than her picture on the cigarette case but it was unmistakably her. Pepper was standing behind the chair with both hands on Sarah's shoulders.

I leaned over and quietly said, "Miss Bennett? Can you walk?"

She looked up and whispered. "Yes, I can walk. I think my bag and purse are in another room. Could you get them?"

I nodded to Murph and he left."

"Pepper, help her get dressed."

I turned my back to them and looked at Dresner. "Turn around and face the wall."

He did. I checked on Helmut. He had his eyes closed and was whimpering. If his eyes hadn't been closed, I'd have kicked him again.

I heard a moan from the floor. Smith Number One was waking up. My slug had caught him under the left rib cage and might have clipped a lung. I wasn't sure. The blood was bright red, though it was oozing, not pouring out. I walked over, relieved him of his automatic that was still in his shoulder rig and then prodded him with my foot. "Wake up! Wake up or I'll put a bullet in your crotch."

He woke up. I told him to crawl over next to his buddy, Stephen, who was against the wall. He slid more than crawled, leaving a six inch wide smear of blood on the floor.

Murph came back in with Sarah's suitcase and purse and handed them to Pepper who shouldered the bag and put the purse under her arm.

I went back to Sarah who was now dressed. "Do you need to go to a hospital, Miss Bennett?"

She was shivering. "I-I-I don't know."

"Would you rather go to Ariella Blumfeld's first and then decide?"

"Oh yes . . . Please."

I turned and said, "Dresner! Who has the keys to the Checker outside?"

"Helmut."

I went to Helmut, fished the keys from his pants pocket which were still around his ankles and handed them to Pepper. I gave her Ari's address, asked her to repeat it, and then said, "Take Miss Bennett outside, collect Herb and Jake, and take her to Ari's in the cab. Either of them knows the city well so whichever wants to drive, that's fine."

As she was helping Sarah to her feet, she asked, "What are you going to do with this bunch?"

"I'm working on it. I'll tell you what I decided when I get to Ari's."

"I'd kill all three of them."

"That's one option."

As they were going out the door I noticed a puddle of urine forming at the feet of Dresner. I smiled at Murph and pointed. He nodded and asked, "Do you want to kill them or should I?"

I almost laughed out loud. "I have a better idea."

I walked over to Dresner and turned him around to face me. "You're going to do exactly as I say. Do you understand?"

He nodded yes.

"Say it!"

"Yes."

"You're going to clean this mess up. I don't care how. Take these two to a hospital or kill them or leave them here to bleed to death. Your choice. Now, here's the important part. You, Dresner, have forty-eight hours to get out of the country and never return. And I suggest you take these two with you if they're still alive in a few hours."

I put my .45 under his chin and forced it up. "Now hear this and believe it. I found Sarah Bennett. I can find you no matter where you run to. If you're not out of the country in forty-eight hours, I'll track you down and kill you. Understand?"

"Yes. Wh-Wh-What about John?"

"John is the least of your worries. I'll see to him."

I looked at Murph and nodded toward the door. We were half way down the corridor when he asked, "What about the guy we taped up outside?"

"That's John. We'll turn him loose in a way he won't know who we are. I don't think he's much more than a messenger boy."

When we got into the garage area, Ari's brother was still sitting against the wall where we left him. We walked over to him and stood him up.

I turned on my hard guy gravel voice again. "Here's what's going to happen. We're going to remove the cuffs and the tape over your mouth. The tape will remain over your eyes till you've walked thirty paces straight ahead. At that point, you can remove the tape yourself. If you make any attempt to turn around, I'll shoot you. Understand?"

He nodded.

Murph removed the cuffs and peeled the tape off his mouth with a snap that turned his head part way around. He let out a gasp. We pointed him toward the doors.

"Let me say this again. If you make the slightest turn after walking thirty paces, I'll shoot you in the back. As soon as you can see, you run for the door, go through it and keep running. And if you're smart, you'll get out of town because if you don't, I may put a bullet in your gut next time I see you. Got it?"

"Yeah. Got it. What happened to the others?"

"You don't want to know. Now start walking. Don't look back!"

He did exactly as told, but when he pulled off the tape that covered his eyes, he gave out a small scream, then dropped the tape before he took off at a run for the door. We walked to where the tape was laying on the floor and I picked it up. There were two sets of eyebrows stuck to it. We both chuckled.

TWENTY NINE

We walked back to the deli, called a cab, and had a cup of coffee while we waited. Murph hadn't said much while we walked but after we sat at a table with our coffee he turned to me with a smile.

"It was a good night's work, Max."

"It was, Murph, it was. I wish we could have pulled it off without any shooting, but God knows, all those bastards deserved to be shot."

"Aye, and there was no choice, lad. Two of the four had guns in their hands, one was preoccupied but armed, and the bastard in charge probably would have used a gun if he had one. You got lucky with that ricochet."

"Tell me about it. I could have followed up with a second shot but I was moving fast enough and saw he hadn't cleared the automatic from his holster so I slammed him in the head with my .45 as we fell. But you're right. We were lucky all the way around."

"Pepper's shot was what you might call optional."

I laughed. "Yeah, but a worthy one. The guy raping Miss Bennett deserved worse. He was at just enough of an angle that I think her shot went through both buttocks. If he lives, he's going to have an unhappy reminder every time he sits down."

Our cab arrived and I gave him Ari's address. It was snowing again, not hard but steady. The snow prompted thoughts of Christmas just a few days away. I'd have to get something nice for Ari. Probably smart to talk to Pepper about it.

Jake came to the front door less than a minute after I rang the buzzer. He was smiling and said, "Everything seems okay up stairs. Kinda crowded but Herb and I will be leaving in a few minutes. Miss Blumfeld took over the care of Miss Bennett and I think is helping her with a bath. Your partner is still here as well."

Pepper was sitting on the couch sipping a glass of wine when we came into the apartment. She smiled and tipped the glass to me. "Good night's work, boss."

"You're the second person to say that to me. I agree. Where's our damsel in distress?"

"In the tub, or maybe out of it by now. Ari said she thinks she'll be alright after she's clean inside and out, and is in bed. She'll probably have a bumpy ride emotionally for a while, but she strikes me as a strong woman, so she'll get over it."

I could hear voices down the hallway and thought about walking back to see Sarah Bennett but decided to wait for Ari. In the meantime, I walked over to Jake and Herb who were standing by the front door.

I pulled out my wallet and handed each one of them a twenty dollar bill. "You fellows did a fine job this evening, one you can be proud of, but I think it would be smart not to mention it to anyone. I don't think there will be any problems but it would be a good idea to let things settle for a few days and watch the newspapers for any report of our fun and games this evening. You can take off now but stay in touch."

After they'd gone I wandered into the kitchen and found a couple beers in the refrigerator, one for me and one for Murph. We were sitting in the living room sipping when Ari came in.

"She's in my bed and would like to see you, Max."

"How is she?"

"Tired. Emotionally shaken, but I think she'll be alright."

I walked down the hallway and tapped on Ari's bedroom door.

"Come in."

She was propped up on a couple pillows and wearing Ari's robe. Her face was pale but with a bit of color in her cheeks. The hot bath had probably helped. I stood at the end of the bed.

She smiled. She had a nice smile. "So you're my knight in shining armor, huh?"

"Nah. Just a guy looking for some excitement on a quiet evening."

She chuckled. "Not according to Ari. She said once you started looking for me you wouldn't give up till you found me. I owe you my life. I'm sure they were going to kill me whether I gave them what they wanted or not."

I didn't sugarcoat it. "I'm certain they planned to kill you. To be honest, I'm surprised they didn't do it within a day or two of kidnapping you. Why was that?"

"Dresner, who was the controller of my two watchers, was out of town. South America, according to one of the Smiths. He didn't get back till this morning and came to my cell this afternoon. I knew when he came in that it was all over. While I'm thinking of it, did a Hans

Moller get in touch with you? Is that why you started looking for me?"

"Moller is dead. But in a sense, it was Moller who started my search. He'd been shot and I found him. His dying words were to find you."

"I didn't care much for the man but I'm sorry to hear he died. I'm glad it was you he spoke to. Was it the men who held me that killed him?"

"No, it doesn't appear that way. The police think it was just a random stickup that went bad. Not that it would do them much good now, but did those bastards in the warehouse get what they wanted?"

"No. Part is in my head and part is sewn into the tongues of my boots. They didn't get either."

"You're a helluva brave lady, Miss Bennett."

"And Ari's got a helluva brave man, Mr. Grant." She was smiling again. "She's in love with you, you know."

I was smiling as well. "Jesus! There are no secrets in the world anymore."

"Oh yes there are!"

"Well, my feeling is the same toward Ari. On another subject, I promised I'd phone Professor Fielding this evening. I'll tell him you'll get in touch with him tomorrow. That okay?"

"That'll be fine. Tell him I'll call him in the morning."

"Back to the subject of Moller. We found a couple small sheets of thin paper rolled up in two Camel cigarettes that were in a cigarette case I took from him. The case had a picture of you on the front. A bit risqué, I might add."

She blushed. "I think I know the photo you're talking about. A rash decision out of my past, but I must add that it paid my way to England and then some. Did you look at the papers?"

"We did."

"We?"

"My associate Pepper and myself. Pepper is the woman who shot the fellow in the ass who was holding you."

"Holding? You're being kind."

I smiled. "I know. We couldn't make much out of what was written on the papers but it seemed to refer to a substitute for heavy water, whatever that is. The only heavy water I've come in contact with is the kind that has bourbon added to it."

She chuckled. "Heavy water is used in the nuclear fission process but to make it is time consuming and resource intensive. Do you still have the papers?"

"Yes, locked up."

"If you could get them to me tomorrow, I'll give them to my contact at the institute along with mine."

"Either Pepper or myself will bring them tomorrow morning."

"That'll work. You bring them. Ari would like that."

I turned to leave. "Good night, Miss Bennett."

"Sarah."

"Good night, Sarah."

When I got back to the living room, Murph had gone, but left the two wallets on the table he'd taken from Smith Number One and Dresner. Pepper said he'd call me at the office sometime tomorrow. Ari kissed me on the cheek and said she'd be right back after she checked to see if there was anything Sarah needed. While she was gone, I asked Pepper for some help on a Christmas present for Ari.

She said, "Let me think about it. I'll let you know tomorrow at the office."

"Speaking of letting someone know, I'd better phone Professor Fielding. I have to call Belden as well but that can wait till I get back to my place."

I took the piece of paper with Fielding's number from my shirt pocket and dialed. He must have been sitting on the phone because he got it half way through the first ring.

"Fielding here."

"Professor, this is Max Grant. We have Sarah Bennett."

The relief in his voice was patent. "Oh, thank God. Is she okay?"

"She's exhausted, physically and emotionally, but I think she'll be alright. She's a tough lady."

"Did you have any trouble?"

"A bit but I won't go into that now. Let's just say that the men who kidnapped her won't be doing a repeat performance for a while, if ever. Right now, she's at Ariella Blumfeld's apartment. She did say she'd phone you at the Institute in the morning."

"You've done an excellent job, Mr. Grant. Thank you."

"You're welcome. Sarah has some information for you, some on papers she had hidden. We discovered some papers in Moller's effects as well. We'll bring them to Sarah tomorrow morning and she'll hand everything over to you when you meet. Also, we had some additional expenses, not extraordinary, but unplanned."

"Whatever they are, we'll gladly take care of them. I must call Professor von Neumann. Thank you again, Mr. Grant."

Ari came back. "She's sleeping. I'll bed down on the couch tonight and call in tomorrow for a day off. They won't like the short notice, but I'll tell them I'm sick if I need to." She paused for a moment. "Pepper told me everything that happened. Just listening was frightening."

I had debated telling Ari about her brother. There were a lot of pros and cons. I could keep it a secret but secrets have a way of surfacing and could ruin our relationship is she discovered his involvement and found I hadn't said anything about it. I doubted any explanation at that point would make things right.

"Ari, there's one thing Pepper didn't know. Your brother was there." I looked at Pepper. "He was the guy who came out the door when you were behind the Checker cab and pointed the gun at you." I turned to Ari. "He's alright. We let him go but hopefully, scared the hell out of him. He didn't see my face or Murph's so he doesn't know who tied him up and blindfolded him. I'd just as soon he never finds out."

Ari looked stricken. "You mean he was going to shoot Pepper?"

"He never had the chance. We were on him from behind before he could decide what he wanted to do. That doesn't mean he wouldn't have if we'd been slower, but Pepper was pretty well protected by the cab. It's a good thing he didn't. Pepper would have shot back. She doesn't miss. But none of that happened. The last time we saw him he was running for the garage door and the alley. I threatened to shoot him if he looked back or if I saw him again. I wouldn't unless pressed, but he doesn't know that."

Ari said, "My God, I knew he was active in the Bund but I had no idea . . . He'd better never come here again."

I fished in my pocket for my pipe and tobacco. "If he does, I suggest you don't mention that you know anything about what happened tonight. I strongly suggested he get out of town and I think he may do that. He got some money from you a couple days ago to go to Germany. I'll bet he goes."

The door buzzer sounded, one long and one short. Ari looked at me. "That's him! That little bastard! I'll—"

I cut her off. "No, honey, just let him in. See what he wants. Don't let on you know anything about what happened this evening."

She put her hand to her face. "Okay, Max, I'll try."

She went to the stairs and in a couple minutes she was back with her brother. He was no sooner in the living room when he demanded, "I need money. Cash. Any that you have here. I cashed your check yesterday but need extra because I'm leaving New York tomorrow morning." That's when he saw us. "Who are these people?"

Ari said, "Just friends."

He looked straight at Pepper. "You mean you let a nigger in here? You got nigger friends?"

That did it. I stood, took three long steps, grabbed him by the front of his jacket and ran him backwards, slamming him into the front door.

"You're leaving! Now!"

I opened the front door, shoved him and followed him out to the steps. He almost fell on the first step but caught himself and said, "Who the fuck do you think you are?"

"Your worst nightmare, sonny, now get the hell out of here!"

I turned him around and gave him a shove. He stumbled down a couple steps and slowed like he was going to turn around and say something.

In a gravelly voice like the one I'd used at the warehouse, I said, "Don't look back."

He stopped as though he'd hit a brick wall but didn't turn around. "You son of a bitch!"

"You got that right, sweetheart. Bon voyage."

EPILOGUE

Morning came early, or at least earlier than I wanted it to. I had called a taxi for Pepper and myself the night before, dropped her off and then returned to my cave for a stiff bourbon before hitting the sack. Better than a sleeping pill, or usually is. Not last night. I tossed and turned for an hour before drifting off. It doesn't take a scientist to know it takes a while for the adrenaline to wear off and the mind to calm down. But the action at the warehouse wasn't the only thing my subconscious was playing games with. Ari and I were both serious about our relationship but how serious only time would tell. Problem is, the mind races ahead leapfrogging all the steps between step one and step ten. I was having visions of tuxedos and wedding gowns. Slow down, Max. Ya got a lot of ground to cover yet.

I was up and about too early to wait on the kid from the deli for coffee, so I put a pot on, then headed to the bathroom for my morning routine. I finished about the same time the coffee quit perking. At least my timing was good even if I was moving in slow motion.

Just shy of seven o'clock and still in my robe, I was pouring a cup of coffee when the phone rang. I couldn't imagine it was business.

"Max Grant."

"Larry Belden. Thanks again for calling me last night. I thought you'd like to know that two men, both named Smith, were treated for gunshot wounds at the Methodist Hospital just a few blocks east of Red Hook. One was treated for a grazing shot that broke a rib, and released. The other, who was shot through both buttocks was admitted. Neither were saying much. The story they told is, they were out for a walk when someone they couldn't identify came out of an alley and started shooting. We won't be able to shake their story. Who shot the guy in the ass?"

"Pepper. He was in the process of raping Sarah Bennett. Pepper didn't take kindly to that. Put one round in his ass and if he hadn't fallen to the side, I think she would have put another in him higher up, but she saw he was out of the way and rushed to put a blanket over Miss Bennett."

"Remind me to be all smiles around Pepper."

I chuckled. "She's tame most of the time."

"Speaking of shootings, some clown shot himself in the foot at the Brooklyn docks. He was trying to board the S.S. Rex, one of the ships of the Italia Line headed for Genoa, without a ticket or passport. When challenged by security, he tried to pull a gun from his pocket and it went off. Some young wacko dressed in a German Bund uniform. They took him to the same hospital as the Smiths."

I had a feeling . . . "Do you have a name?"

"Wait a minute." I could hear him shuffling papers. "Yeah, here it is. Gave his name as Vogel. John Vogel. Know him?"

"Doesn't ring a bell. Sounds like a real klutz. Don't give his gun back."

"Oh, he won't get it back. He's handcuffed to his bed and will be charged with a number of felonies—deadly assault, carrying a handgun without a permit, and several others. He'll spend some time in the Tombs and probably Sing-Sing if the judge is in a foul mood."

"Serves him right. He ought to be charged with stupidity."

"If that was a legitimate charge, we'd have to build ten new prisons."

"One more thing, Larry. I have three wallets that might interest you. I'll drop them off at the station tomorrow or the next day."

"Okay, I gotta go. See ya around, Max."

"Yeah, Larry. Thanks for the call."

Now what? Call Ari? No . . . Get dressed and think about it. If her brother gave Ari as next of kin or someone to contact, they'd have done it already and I think she would have called, but she hadn't. So the asshole had kept his mouth shut. Just as well. He'd had an embarrassing evening and from the looks of it, Hitler was going to have to fight his war without the help of Johan Blumfeld, alias John Vogel. Even if he'd managed to get to Germany, someone, somehow, would have eventually discovered he was Jewish and that would be the end of him. I felt nothing but animosity toward him but he was Ari's brother and would be safer in prison than following his idiotic scheme of fighting for the fatherland. Maybe some tried and true American criminals could straighten him out.

I got dressed, left my sportcoat off but strapped on my shoulder rig with my snubnose in it. I was beginning to feel naked without it but didn't like the feeling that it was necessary to carry it. I could wean myself of it over a few days or a week but the problem is the one time

I might need it, it would be in the safe. That had happened recently. Ah well . . .

I was standing behind my desk lighting my pipe when Pepper came in, followed by Bo, followed by the boy from the deli. I was beginning to think charging admission might be another source of income when Bo strolled into my office and sat in the chair next to my desk. The chair creaked in pain.

"Was Pepper in any danger last night, Mr. Grant? I don' like it if Pepper is in danger of gettin' hurt."

Man, I wasn't about to get on this giant's shit list! "No, Bo, she wasn't. I take it she told you about it. If anyone was in any danger, it was the scuzzballs in front of her. She shot one in the ass and would have plugged him again if he hadn't fallen out of the way."

"Well, I wouldn't take kindly to anyone who hurt her or put her in a fix where she'd get hurt."

Jesus! I wouldn't take kindly to him not feeling kindly. "Look, Bo, she's very important to me and I'd never ask her to take on a job that would get her hurt. It was her idea to go along because it was a woman who was being held captive. Pepper was right. It was a good decision on her part and we needed her. Even the cop who knew what we did thought she was a hero."

Hero in so many words, I thought.

He smiled. "Hero, huh? That's nice. Okay. I gotta be going. Gotta do some Christmas shopping for my hero."

He got up. I got up. I looked up. He stuck out his hand and buried my hand in his. I didn't wince till after he left.

Pepper came in, Danish in one hand and coffee in the other. "I couldn't stop him from coming in with me. I told him about last night and he said he wanted to be sure you weren't putting me in any danger."

"I told him straight. The ones in danger were the bastards at thc warehouse. I really did think you were going to shoot that other Smith again. Glad you didn't."

"I would have if he hadn't moved away from Sarah."

"Yeah, I figured . . ." I sat back down and went on to tell her about Sergeant Belden's phone call and that both Smiths had made it to the hospital. I didn't say anything about Ari's brother.

"I'm leaving for Ari's in a few minutes. I'll take the cigarette case and papers we found in the cigarettes. By the way, have you thought of anything I could get for Ari for Christmas?"

"I think so. When's her birthday?"

"I don't know."

"Find out. A nice gold chain with a birthstone pendant and matching earrings would make a fine gift. I'm sure she'd love it."

"Ah . . . sparkling idea. Literally. I'll find out."

I picked up the phone and dialed Ari's number.

"Hello?"

"Hi Ari, it's Max. How's your patient?"

"She's feeling much better. Just had another bath, breakfast, and I think about a half pot of coffee."

"Sounds good. I'm going to come to your place and bring some papers for her. I should be there in about a half hour. Okay?"

"Yes. I need a hug."

"You'll get one. Promise."

I took a cab and in less than thirty minutes I was following Ari upstairs to her apartment, after a hug at the front door, of course.

Sarah Bennett was sitting in the chair across from the couch in the living room. She started to rise but I just motioned her down and took a seat on the couch across from her.

I handed her the cigarette case. "That's what started my search for you."

She took it, blushed slightly, and smiled. "Sometimes things we do early in life come back to haunt us. This time, it saved my life."

She took the papers from the case, pressed them flat on the coffee table and studied them for a few minutes. "I know you may not understand, but these papers make a strong case for using graphite as a moderator instead of heavy water. They complement the papers I have. The purpose of a moderator is to slow down neutrons to thermal velocities by collisions. As a result, the neutrons are able to fission with Uranium 235 and cause a self-sustaining reaction."

I looked at her for a few seconds, then said, "I think I'll stick to bourbon as a moderator."

She laughed, as did Ari who was now sitting next to me.

Sarah put the papers together and picked up the case. "May I keep this?"

"Sure," I said, smiling, "I have the original."

"You're kidding!"

"Nope. I have to give it back to Rubin Stein but I'm sure he'd make a copy for me if I wanted one." I looked at Ari. "I don't think I will, though."

Sarah stood up. "I'm going to phone the Institute. Be right back."

I turned to Ari. "I have some interesting news about your brother. Last night, he tried to force his way aboard a ship bound for Italy. When security stopped him, he pulled a gun but it caught on his pocket and he shot himself in the foot."

Her mouth dropped open. "You can't be serious."

"I am. He was arrested and taken to a hospital where they patched him up and handcuffed him to his bed. He'll be charged with several felonies and most probably be convicted. The upshot of it all is that it's doubtful he'll make it to Germany for at least a couple years."

She stared at me for a minute and then burst out laughing. "That's wonderful! I mean, it's not wonderful that he shot himself, but maybe in a couple years he'll have changed his mind about some things. Max, I love you!"

I was laughing, too. "Hell, I didn't shoot him."

"No, but you're cause and effect."

"Speaking of cause and effect—I left my toothbrush and shave kit here, didn't I?"

"Yes. And Sarah is checking into her hotel this afternoon."

"Hmmm . . . one more thing. When is your birthday?

END